I0665401

Other books by Michael Bracken

Fiction

Bad Girls
Deadly Campaign
Even Roses Bleed
In the Town of Dreams Unborn and Memories Dying
Just in Time for Love
Psi Cops
Tequila Sunrise

ALL WHITE GIRLS

Michael Bracken

WILDSIDE PRESS
Berkeley Heights, New Jersey

All White Girls
A publication of
Wildside Press
P.O. Box 45
Gillette, NJ 07933-0045
www.wildsidepress.com

FIRST EDITION

to SHARON
with love always

to PAMELA
forever in heart and mind

Chapter 1

The brim of Rickenbacher's battered fedora hung low over his left eye as he shouldered his way through the late-evening crowd milling about on the sidewalk in front of a three-block long stretch of strip joints and pornographic book stores. The hat — a half-size too small and tight at his temples — hid his thinning hair and the bald spot he'd rediscovered that morning.

He pushed his way into the Muff Inn, dropped onto a stool as far from the entrance as possible, and ordered a three-dollar beer. It was the beginning of a long, dirty night, the kind of night where winos met God and hookers dreamed of saying, "Not tonight, dear, I have a headache" to some missionary-position-only working stiff in a suburban split-level.

"What's all the commotion outside?" the unfamiliar bartender asked as he dropped an unopened beer bottle in front of Rickenbacher.

"Some sleaze tried to swallow the sidewalk."

When Rickenbacher failed to elaborate, the bartender shrugged and moved away.

The young woman on the stage behind the bar, her heavy breasts already scarred by stretch marks from an explosive spurt of growth during her late teens, turned her back to the men watching her, bent, and peeled away her red silk panties. They caught on one of her spike heels and she almost toppled over as she momentarily lost her balance. Then, having given the men an intimate look at her young body, she turned again to face them.

And she moved, but not quite to the music. Each thrust of her hips, each bump and grind, each jiggle of her breasts, was an ungainly movement like she'd only recently developed neuromotor skills. The men in the audience didn't seem to care as they drank their beer and stared at whichever body part held their fascination.

For Rickenbacher it was the eyes, the clouded eyes that focused on nothing and shimmered with unshed tears. Down the street were the professionals, the slender women who danced the dance, the women who performed as if each performance were a Broadway audition. Here were the girls with nowhere else to turn.

As the song ended, the dancer scooped up her discarded clothing, crushing the wad of cloth against her breasts, and hurried off-stage. A malnourished blonde replaced her.

Rickenbacher downed the last of his beer and rubbed his bruised knuckles. Before the blonde finished disrobing, a uniformed police officer stepped into the strip joint, squinted against the bright stage lights, and then slowly walked down the length of the bar toward Rickenbacher.

"There's a dead guy outside," the officer said.

Rickenbacher stood and followed the cop out of the bar to where a handful of gawkers stared at a dead man's body sprawled in a pool of shattered glass.

A neon cacophony hung only a few feet above their heads, the popping and buzzing of the lights only occasionally drowned out by the shouts of the barkers, bulbous men whose doughy fat strained at their sweat-stained t-shirts as they called out, "Girls! All White Girls!" and "Biggest tits on the block!" and "Take a look, gentlemen! None Better!

None Finer! None Younger!"

"You know him?" the cop asked.

"I met him once."

"A couple of these guys say they saw you coming out of that door a few minutes ago." Glass crunched under the cop's shoes as he turned to indicate a door wedged between two buildings, unlit and without advertisement. "The stairs inside lead up to his office."

Rickenbacher shrugged.

"Don't talk much, do you?" The cop took off his hat and held it in his left hand as he ran the thin fingers of his right hand through his closely cropped blond hair. He'd been walking this beat only three months and already he'd seen more dead bodies than he'd seen his entire first year on the force when he'd been teamed with a career sergeant named Kowalski and had walked a beat in the yuppie district.

"The Lieutenant been called yet?"

"Yeah," the officer said. The radio on his hip squawked as if to answer. "He'll be here."

The winos and the street people turned away from the body or stepped around it. Only the tourists and the conventioneers still stared, nudging each other and whispering questions.

Rickenbacher wore a faded beige London Fog trench coat, had a recently-acquired file-folder buried deep inside one of the pockets, and he reached into a different pocket for a pack of cigarettes. He shook one loose, wrapped his thick lips around the filter, and pulled it free. Then he held the nearly empty pack out to the cop and had his offer rejected with a quick shake of the young man's head. He slid the cigarettes back into his pocket and retrieved a butane lighter, snapping it to life and cupping his hand around the flame to shield it from the still-born breeze.

An unmarked car pulled to the curb as Rickenbacher sucked the flame against the end of his cigarette. A gaunt man with thick black hair greying at the temples opened the door and walked around to the sidewalk in front of Ricken-bacher. He wore a coat like the bigger man and it hung open to reveal a crisp white shirt and a narrow black tie held in place by a gold tie chain.

"Dick," he said with a nod.

"Lieutenant." Rickenbacher responded with his own nod.

Lieutenant Salvador Castellano stepped past him, took the uniformed officer by the elbow, and talked quietly with him for the next five minutes. Then he returned to Ricken-bacher.

"How'd it happen?"

Rickenbacher pulled the cigarette from between his lips and held it military style, the filter between his thumb and forefinger, the glowing end in the cup of his hand. "He tripped."

The Lieutenant looked up at the broken window, then down at the body. It wasn't a long fall, but the sudden impact had broken the man's neck. "Self-defense?"

"He tripped," Rickenbacher repeated.

"What happened to your knuckles?"

Rickenbacher took a long drag from his cigarette, letting the Lieutenant get a good look at the discoloring skin. "Hit a door."

"We find out different, you be around?"

"You know where."

"Yeah," the Lieutenant said as Rickenbacher turned away. "I know where."

"She a virgin?" Paul Canfield motioned toward the young woman standing next to Bleach. She could have been any age from fourteen to twenty-four, with make-up thick on her face as if it had been applied with a putty knife, and long black hair that cascaded down to the middle of her back. She wore a blood-red tube top that revealed more of her firm young breasts than it concealed, a tight-fitting black leather miniskirt, sheer black pantyhose, and red fuck-me pumps with spike heels. Her nervous eyes darted from one man to the other as they spoke, but she said nothing.

"Guaranteed," said the slim mulatto. The fine spray of freckles across the bridge of his nose was visible in daylight, but rarely seen by those who knew him. Bleach only came out at night.

"How do you know?"

"I plucked her from the bus station myself."

A tan sedan cruised past but the two men ignored it. It turned left at the corner and disappeared from sight.

"What's she been doing?"

"Hand jobs. She's intact," Bleach said. "Not even a Tampax up there."

"Her ass?"

"Yeah."

"How much?"

"Five hundred."

Canfield peeled ten fifties off a roll he retrieved from the right front pocket of his tight-fitting jeans and handed them to the other man. Bleach smiled — a small tight smile that barely moved the corners of his thick lips — as he placed the bills in his wallet and slid the wallet into the inside breast pocket of his jacket.

Bleach grabbed the girl's elbow and pulled her aside. He whispered harshly into her ear. "This be my man," he said. "You treat him right. You don't, you know what's gonna happen."

She nodded quickly and Bleach released his grip on her elbow. He'd only hit her once — a backhand across the face that caught her attention — but she'd seen what he'd done to one of the other girls with an electrical cord. The whipping had been so bad the girl had been unable to work for a week, and when she did return to the street no amount of make-up had been able to cover the welts and the scabs, and her earnings had been dangerously low.

After Bleach left them, Canfield took the girl to a room he'd already rented at the Grafenberg Hotel — a room with water stains on the ceiling, a television which received only two channels, and a bed with a brand-new mattress. He had insisted on a good mattress.

"Wash your face," Canfield demanded as soon as he locked the door behind them.

She stood by the bed, her fingers already fumbling with the zipper on the back of her skirt.

"Now," Canfield demanded quietly. When she hesitated, he took her arm and propelled her toward the bathroom. "Don't come back out until you've washed all that shit off your face."

Canfield waited until he heard water running in the sink, then he peeled off his pale blue polo shirt, revealing the thick muscles on his arms, his slim waist, and the snake tattoo over his left nipple that danced when he tensed his pectorals.

He pulled back the thin beige cover and the off-white top sheet, revealing faded blood stains in the middle of the bottom sheet, stains from a previous guest that hadn't completely bleached away. Two thin foam pillows had been knocked askew when he'd pulled away the covers, and he straightened them. The double-bed had no headboard, but on either side of it stood a night stand. Each night stand had a single drawer and into the drawer nearest him, next to the never-opened copy of Gideon's Bible, Canfield placed the switchblade he wore inside his left boot.

After sitting on the edge of the mattress, he pulled off his black, silver-toed cowboy boots and placed them next to the bed. Into each boot went the corresponding sock. Then he popped open each button of his black button-fly Levi's, peeled the jeans off, folded them, and lay them in the room's only chair. He wore no underwear.

The girl stepped from the bathroom, still wiping her face dry with one of the bath towels.

"How's this?" she asked cautiously. Her voice carried the inflections of a person born and raised far south of the Mason-Dixon line.

Canfield turned to face her and saw what the thick layer of make-up had hidden, that age had not etched even one line in the delicate skin of her face.

"How old are you?"

"Sixteen." She bit at her bottom lip. "I'll be seventeen tomorrow."

"Pretty damn old to be a virgin."

Her shrug was barely perceptible.

"Take your clothes off."

She reached behind herself and finished undoing the leather miniskirt. It dropped to the floor at her feet. She pulled the tube top up, over her head and off, letting it fall to the floor with the leather mini, then she stepped out of her skirt and out of her pumps. She rolled her black panty-hose from her hips and down her thighs, until she could step out of them.

She stood facing Canfield and waited.

"Get on the bed."

The girl sat on the edge of the bed, then pushed herself into the center and lay back. Canfield joined her a moment later, kneeling between her legs. He grabbed her thighs and pulled her to him as he forced himself into her. She was tight and dry and he buried himself deeper and deeper.

She struggled, but Canfield completely covered her, pinning her to the bed with his weight. He covered her mouth with his and tasted the blood where she'd bitten her own tongue to keep from screaming.

He pulled back and drove into her mechanically. Then he pulled out of her and she caught her breath.

"Roll over."

He twisted the girl onto her belly, then pulled her up onto her knees. He took her from behind and this time she screamed. The sound penetrated the thin walls into the surrounding rooms, but screams — like sirens — were so common in the neighborhood that no one ever heard them.

He held onto her hips and drove into her, thrusting faster and faster until he could no longer restrain himself. He released into her, held her tight until the throbbing stopped, and then he pulled away.

She collapsed on the bed, crying silently, her tears staining the pillow she'd buried her face into.

Canfield stood beside the bed. "Roll over and sit up."

When she hesitated, he gripped her arm, forcing her over and then up into a sitting position. She stared at her feet, her hair hanging around her face. Canfield caught her chin between his thumb and his forefinger and forced her to look up at him.

"Now lick it clean."

She hesitated again, so he slipped his switchblade from the night stand, snapped it open, and pressed the point against the soft underside of her jaw. She opened her mouth and took him in, gagging as a tiny bubble of blood appeared around the knife point.

Afterward, he showered and dressed, wiped his knife blade clean on one of the wet towels, then slipped the switchblade back into his left boot before opening the hotel room door and stepping into the hall.

Just before he closed the door, Canfield looked back at the girl on the bed.

"Happy birthday," he said.

Rickenbacher didn't want to return to his empty apartment and another evening of black-and-white reruns from the fifties and sixties. He didn't love Lucy and he wouldn't leave it to Beaver. Instead, he drove, windows open to let the grimy city air curl around his face and tickle what remained of his hair.

His trench coat lay on the seat beside him, his fedora covering it. He'd rolled up his shirt sleeves and he drove with his left arm resting on the open window frame, his elbow jutting out. A cigarette dangled from the corner of his mouth, ash whipped away by the breeze as it grew too heavy at the burning end. He sucked on it, blew the residue smoke through his nose, and reached for the radio to improve the reception on a station that kept fading in and out.

He turned off the main street, away from the rental cars and low-riders that claimed the avenue, away from the restaurants and nightclubs that attracted the crowds, away from the bright lights and into the darkness. He cut off a late model Eldorado and the driver, a balding fat man wearing too many gold chains, gave him an upraised middle finger in return.

Parked cars crowded both sides of the street, apartment and tenement residents fighting for parking space because their buildings lacked garages. The cars were beaters — city cars dented and scratched, with broken windows and missing antennas, balding tires and sagging springs, empty holes in trunks where locks had once been, bumper stickers used more to cover rust than to convey messages.

Rickenbacher didn't pay any attention to the street before him as he fiddled with the radio to tune in a plaintive Janis Joplin song, and he missed the corner stop sign hidden behind a parked delivery truck. A woman jogged out in front of Rickenbacher and he glanced up just in time to slam on the brakes. His van lurched to a stop inches from her.

The woman turned to him as she ran slowly past, glaring at him but unable to see into the darkness of the van. The sight of her face burned Rickenbacher's memory like acid. He hadn't expected to see her again, had never intended to see her again, had no reason to see her again. Yet, there she was, jogging past him, her heavy breasts bouncing with each stride despite the tight-fitting sports bra, the cheeks of her ass slapping together under her sweat pants, her dishwater blonde hair pulled back in a loose pony tail, her face bathed in sweat. Twice before she'd entered his life and twice before she'd left it.

Jesse.

And then she was gone, swallowed by the darkness before he could call out her name.

As one of the city's invisible horde of delivery people, no one ever glanced at Kat a second time when she breezed past. She wore her hair cut into a wedge so that it wouldn't blow around under her bicycle helmet, rarely wore make-up because the wind and the rain wrecked havoc with it and gave her a clown's mask, and during the month she'd had the job she'd turned a layer of fat into hardening muscle that her knee-length biker shorts and her skin-tight sports bra failed to conceal.

As the elevator doors closed, she saw the man exiting room 4B, but she didn't pay much attention to him, her gaze sliding over his face, the gloved hand gripping the door knob, and the bulge in the pocket of his overcoat. A greasy-haired blond with an upside-down cross tattooed on the back of his left hand had just pissed her off by closing his hotel room door in her face without tipping her and without so much as a thank you. The city had more than its share of creeps and she seemed to meet most of them.

The man exiting 4B carefully pulled the door shut and,

unaware that he'd been seen, walked quietly to the staircase, taking the stairs down two at a time until he reached the ground floor. He had disappeared before the aging elevator wheezed open and Kat made her way outside to the ten speed mountain bike she'd chained to a hydrant.

Chapter 2

Rickenbacher suppressed a belch, then rolled over and retrieved the ringing phone from the stand next to his bed. The answering machine in the living room wouldn't pick up until the sixth ring and he didn't want to wait for it. He closed his eyes against the sunlight streaming into his room through a gap between the curtains. Into the receiver, he said, "Rickenbacher."

Hubert Cove identified himself, then asked, "Any luck?"

"Some. Not much."

"You've been at it for a week."

"This is a big city."

"Then make it smaller."

Rickenbacher didn't respond. He suppressed another belch.

"Just find her."

Rickenbacher heard the click as Cove broke the connection. Then he rolled over, replaced the phone on the night stand, and lay on his stomach, his head turned to the side to stare at the broken paneling on his bedroom wall. A moment later he kicked his legs free of the tangled, sweat-stained sheets, then twisted until he sat upright on the edge of the bed. The sudden surge of movement did nothing to still the thunderstorm in his head nor did it quell the hurricane in his gut.

He'd finished an opened bottle of Jack Daniel's he'd found in the cabinet under the kitchen sink when he'd finally returned home the previous evening, mourning a past that he'd long ago tried to forget, and his awakening had reminded Rickenbacher that he wasn't as young and as tough as he'd once been. Lately, he lost more often than he won when he went ten rounds with Jack, and the hangover coursing through his body reminded Rickenbacher that he'd lost another fight.

He pushed himself off the bed and stumbled into the bathroom where he stood under a cold shower for almost half an hour before he made any effort to bathe.

Later, having dressed and having prepared himself a breakfast of lukewarm coffee, Rickenbacher sat at his kitchen table and thumbed through the slim folder of information Hubert Cove had sent. Inside were additional copies of Katherine Cove's high school graduation photo, a newspaper article that listed her as second place winner in a locally-sponsored essay contest, a photocopy of the neatly-typed letter she'd mailed to her father the day she'd left home, and the report a well-known licensed detective agency had prepared for Katherine's father before he'd fired them. Rickenbacher reviewed his notes, the seemingly meaningless jumble of words he'd jotted down to remind himself of the things her father had told him, of the things her high school teachers and friends had told him, and of the things he'd figured out on his own as he'd filtered through everything he'd learned since her father's first phone call.

Katherine had been an average student, though she'd done particularly well in her English classes and always seemed to be reading. She attended church each Sunday with her father, often helping care for the younger children after children's church. She'd dated a few times, but had never gone steady; had a date for Homecoming but not for the Senior Prom. Her friends had figured her to get a job at the new Wal-Mart after graduation and be married with children within five years. What none of them had expected is what had happened. She'd taken a bus to the city using a ticket she'd paid for with money saved from various baby-sitting jobs.

When he closed the folder and tossed it across the kitchen table, Rickenbacher knew no more about Hubert's only child than he had known when he'd looked at every-thing the previous morning. During the week since Cove's original phone call, Rickenbacher had exhausted the obvious sources of information. He'd tracked Katherine's driver's license through the Department of Motor Vehicles, but she'd not submitted a change of address, nor had she ever received any moving violations; he'd tracked her social secu-rity number through both the Social Security Administration and the state's Department of Employment Security, but they had no record of her ever obtaining legitimate employ-ment; neither of the city's two largest credit agencies had any record of her; she'd not obtained a phone in her own name; nor, according to Lieutenant Castellano, had she ever been arrested in the city.

Rickenbacher didn't like dead ends — dead ends had a bad habit of leading to dead people. And he didn't like Hubert Cove. Even though they'd never met, even though all he knew about Cove was the sound of the man's voice, his dislike for incompetent agencies that did little and charged heavily, and the fact that his checks didn't bounce,

Cove grated on his nerves. If he'd been hired for any reason other than the disappearance of Cove's daughter, Rickenbacher would have refunded the advance to be shed of the man.

Instead, he pushed himself away from the table and up from the yellow vinyl kitchen chair, rinsed his coffee mug under cold tap water and set it upside down on a faded dishtowel next to the sink, then retrieved a sky blue windbreaker from the coat closet to pull over his bulky sweater. From his collection of nearly a dozen hats, Rickenbacher selected a dark blue baseball cap devoid of logos and pulled it snug over his head, covering the bald spot whose very presence annoyed him almost as much as Hubert Cove.

The apartment door opened directly to the outside and Rickenbacher carefully secured the dead bolt behind him before looking over the second-floor railing and down at the parking lot where his Pontiac 6000 used to be. Three weeks earlier the car had disappeared during the night and pieces of it had probably made their way from a local chop shop to service stations and auto parts stores all over the midwest. The dark green Dodge van now in his parking space had belonged to his brother-in-law until Rickenbacher had peeled five crumpled hundreds out of his wallet and had taken possession away from the wiry young auto mechanic his sister had married seven years earlier. The van — all he could afford when the insurance company's check did little more than pay off the outstanding loan balance on the Pontiac — had quickly become familiar.

The concrete stairs leading down were halfway between his apartment and the one to his left as he faced the street and he took them two at a time, zipping his windbreaker closed against the late morning chill.

He nodded to Mrs. Stegmann and her obese white poodle as he climbed into the van, then he brought the engine to life and backed out of his parking space. When he pulled into traffic, Rickenbacher pointed the van toward the bus station downtown. One of the two file folders on the passenger seat contained the material he'd obtained from Mr. Johnson's office the night before. In the other were a dozen copies of Katherine's graduation photo. He would show Katherine's photograph around and see if anyone remembered a nervous young blonde from downstate Illinois stepping off a bus six weeks earlier.

And who might have met her or picked her up.

Less than a mile away, someone had turned a hotel room into a Jackson Pollock abstract using only red. Blood red.

Inside the room, officers from the Mobile Crime Scene Unit finished photographing the scene, then called the Emergency Medical Technicians back in to remove the body.

In the hall just outside, a greasy little man stood with Lieutenant Castellano, twitching nervously. "Rosalinda didn't come in today, that's why I was cleaning the rooms. I told her if she misses work one more time I'll fire her. That's what I'll do if she ever comes back. Fire her. I'll bet she doesn't even have a green card. I'll bet —"

The Lieutenant lightly touched the manager's bony shoulder, silencing him. The little man swallowed hard, then pushed his hair off his forehead with one gnarled hand and waited for the Lieutenant's question.

"You touch anything?"

"Just the door when I opened it. It was 11:30. Checkout's at 11:00 but the Do Not Disturb sign was still hanging from the door. I knocked and when nobody answered, I used my pass key to open the door. The drapes were pulled shut so I turned on the light. I didn't see her. I just saw the blood." He pushed his hair away from his face again. "I saw all the blood and then I turned and I saw her on the bed and —"

"You touched the light switch?"

"Yeah, I turned on the light."

"You touch anything else?"

"Nothing. I swear it. I didn't touch nothing."

Two Emergency Medical Technicians wheeled a stretcher out of the room, a full body bag its only occupant. The Grafenberg Hotel's manager turned away, almost gagging when he realized what the body bag contained.

"What did you do then?"

"I backed up, backed right out of the room and pulled the door closed."

"Closed?"

"It wouldn't do for the other guests to see something like that."

"Then?"

"I dialed 911."

"From where?"

"My office. I went straight to my office and dialed 911 and I waited in the lobby until a cop showed up. I took him directly to the room and then I got the hell out of the way like he told me to."

Both men were silent for a moment, then Lieutenant Castellano asked, "Who rented the room?"

"I don't know. He said his name was Marky D. Sod. That's how he registered."

"Did he show you any identification?"

"I didn't ask. Why would I ask? He paid cash up front. Most people do when they come here."

"Do you know who the Marquis de Sade is?"

"Should I?"

The Lieutenant shrugged, then dismissed the nervous little man and stepped into the hotel room where a pair of officers from the Mobile Crime Scene Unit used tongs and tweezers to slip various bits of potential evidence into individual evidence bags, each one labeled like leftovers from a particularly messy holiday gathering. Someone had forced open the room's only window and had propped it up with a Gideon's Bible. Air moved slowly through the opening but a dying city's smog smelled little better than one woman's death and the Lieutenant covered his mouth with his fist and coughed into it.

"Anything?" the Lieutenant asked the taller officer as he leaned against the dresser, his hands at his side, the palm and two fingers of his right hand pressed against the wood.

"Partials on the night stand and all over the bathroom. Lots of fluids, apparently seminal."

"We got a cause of death?"

"Multiple stab wounds to the abdomen and torso, defensive cuts on the dorsal side of her arms where she tried to defend herself. You'll have to wait for the M.E.'s report to confirm what I've just told you."

"Of course," Castellano said. "Where'd she die?"

"On the bed. There's no evidence that the body had been moved after death. There's lividity in her back, buttocks, and the backs of her legs. The sheets and the mattress are blood-soaked and, despite the condition of the room, there's nothing to indicate that the body was transported."

The shorter officer looked up and saw where the Lieutenant's hand rested. "Lieutenant," he said, "we haven't dusted there yet."

Castellano jerked his hand away from the dresser. "Sorry."

At 6'4," Rickenbacher appeared inconspicuous only in a big and tall men's shop; at the bus station he towered over the ticket takers and the bag ladies. He used this advantage to extract answers from even the most reluctant potential witness. Even so, none could identify the girl in the photo he repeatedly displayed for their examination.

"When you say she come through here?" A stringy black man the color and texture of a raisin squinted at the photo, his brow furrowed in concentration. The seventeen-year-old blonde in the photo had since turned eighteen, but to the man holding the photo it didn't matter. He saw a young white woman wearing her best beige blouse. It had been buttoned demurely, revealing no hint of cleavage. She also wore a pair of gold chains around her neck, each bearing a tiny gold cross that nestled in the valley of cloth between her breasts. Her wavy blonde hair had been sun-bleached the color of honey and it cascaded loosely over her shoulders, ending nearly halfway down her back. Her pale blue eyes sparkled and the corners of her lips were pulled up in a coy smile as if she'd remembered the punchline to her favorite joke just as the photographer captured her image on film.

"Month ago," Rickenbacher prompted.

"She pretty. Real pretty." The black man looked up. "Lotsa pretty girls come through here."

"Yeah. This one?"

Shaking his head, the black man returned the photo to Rickenbacher. He'd crumpled the edge and Rickenbacher carefully smoothed the photo as he listened.

"She come through here, I never see her."

Rickenbacher nodded his thanks and moved on.

A moment later a uniformed police officer stopped him. "You've been asking a lot of questions, bothering a lot of people."

Rickenbacher pushed the baseball cap back on his head and waited.

The cop touched Rickenbacher's forearm, unwilling to make a scene when he had no backup, but wanting to encourage the bigger man to cooperate. "I'll have to ask you to leave."

Rickenbacher's gaze slowly swept the interior of the bus depot, taking in the flatulent old women huddled under

layers of Goodwill clothing, the young Puerto Rican pushing
a broom across the broken tile as he bounced to music only
he heard through the headphones of a Walkman radio, and
the trio of adolescent Marines laughing at each other's scato-
logical jokes as they awaited their Greyhound limo back to
camp. Then he walked with the officer toward the glass
doors at the southern end of the building.

As they stepped outside, the officer asked, "What's got
you bugging all these people?"

Rickenbacher showed him the photo of Katherine
Cove.

"Good looking girl." The officer looked up from the
photo. "Your daughter?"

Rickenbacher said she wasn't.

"Then check the stretch. She's probably giving head for
twenty bucks a pop." He laughed as he nudged Rickenbacher
with his elbow. "If you don't find her, you'll find one just
like her."

Rickenbacher stared down at the blue uniform, wondering how long the city had been hiring children to patrol
the streets. Then he pocketed the photo and turned away.

The officer called after him, "This place is like a cherry
tree. We do our best, but we can't keep the pimps from
picking the ripe ones when they arrive."

Rickenbacher had parked his van a block away from the
bus station. On his way to it, he stepped into a noisy diner
and used the pay phone to call Colette Rees and make an
appointment to meet her at the Muff Inn later that afternoon.

Rickenbacher had a list of places to visit after he completed the call, and he began with the nearest one and
worked his way down the list. While he visited the main
offices of the gas, electric, and cable television companies,
the police were busy working on another case involving a
young girl.

In various locations around town, uniformed patrol officers and plainclothes detectives talked to their favorite snitches and collected a motley group of men informally known as the usual suspects, seeking information about the previous evening's murder of a brunette teenager. Within a few hours all but one of the known violent sex offenders had been released, and the remainder waited patiently for yet another interrogation.

The smell of desperation hung in the air like the cloyingly cheap perfume of redneck women. The habitual criminals had long since moved on, leaving only the hard-core alcoholics sleeping off their latest binges and the first-time offenders whose families were too poor to raise bond or post bail.

Lieutenant Castellano walked down the center of the aisle without really noticing the two dozen men crowded into a cell designed for twelve. He'd never seen the holding tank when it wasn't overflowing with society's effluent, and he'd long since passed the point where he noticed or cared. He did notice the wiry blond sitting behind a scarred wooden table in a cramped room on the north side of the building, just past the holding cell. Behind him stood a beefy sergeant whose expansive gut strained the glittering gold buttons of his blue uniform.

The Lieutenant slipped easily into the remaining chair, adjusted the creases on his precisely pressed black slacks as he settled in, and then asked the sergeant without looking at him, "Read him his rights?"

"Twice."

Lieutenant Castellano looked a question at Sergeant Kowalski.

"I don't think he understood me the first time." The sergeant ran a handful of sausage-thick fingers through his closely-cropped salt-and-pepper hair. On the street he had busted heads with his billy and his bare hands long before criminals had rights, but Kowalski had changed with the times and knew just how far he could go before Internal Affairs would question him.

The Lieutenant returned his gaze to the man on the other side of the table. Gilly Boy Thomas stared back through a tangle of greasy blond hair that fell over his forehead and nearly hid his cobalt blue eyes. Gilly Boy's hands were folded neatly on the table before him, his wrists held only inches apart by a pair of stainless steel handcuffs.

"You like to cut women?"

"You've read my sheet," Gilly Boy responded. "I've cut a few." He seemed alert but wary, with no indication that he had any difficulty hearing or understanding the Lieutenant's question.

Lieutenant Castellano had carried a slim manila folder into the room with him and he placed it on the table. From it, he withdrew a pair of 8"x10" glossy photos of the dead woman found at the Grafenberg Hotel and he slid them across the table. "You cut this one?"

Gilly Boy picked up the first photo and examined it closely, the way an art critic might examine a newly discovered van Gogh. He smiled. "No, sir," he said. "But somebody did a damn fine job on the bitch."

"Seen your parole officer lately?"

"Tuesday last," Gilly Boy said as he placed the first photo on the table and picked up the second. His faded jeans grew tight and he made no effort to disguise his pleasure. "She's young."

Lieutenant Castellano retrieved the photos much to Gilly Boy's disappointment and returned them to the folder. The wiry blond watched until the folder snapped shut. The room remained silent save for Kowalski's heavy breathing and the tick of the Lieutenant's index fingernail against the table.

Finally, Gilly Boy asked, "Got any more pictures?"

Lieutenant Castellano pushed himself out of the chair and looked down on the wiry little man. Gilly Boy's prison pallor had disappeared after six months on the outside, but he still bore the crudely etched tattoo of a prison gang on the back of his left hand.

The sergeant cleared his throat. When the Lieutenant looked up at him, Kowalski said, "He says he spent the night at his mother's. She said the same thing."

"Anybody else see him there?"

"The next-door-neighbor came over, spent about fifteen minutes in the same room with him."

Gilly Boy smiled. His alibi had held.

"Cut him loose."

Chapter 3

"Care for a drink?"

"No," Rickenbacher said as he straddled a red leather and chrome stool at the far end of the bar. He'd never finished the beer he'd ordered the previous night. "Thanks."

"On the wagon?"

"That's twelve steps to hell," he said as he dropped a slim file folder on the worn and stained wood before him, still remembering how his head had felt that morning. "I'm just not in the mood."

Carlos, the Muff Inn's regular bartender, shrugged and continued cleaning with the dirty towel he'd pulled from his belt a few minutes earlier. He jerked one thumb over his shoulder at the runway stage behind him and said, "The girls don't start until noon."

"Didn't come for the show."

"No skin off my nose." Carlos lifted both hands in mock-surrender. His English was good, but not his green card, and he didn't need any trouble with the big man.

Rickenbacher sat in silence for almost twenty minutes, watching as the now-mute bartender rearranged bottles, refilling nearly-empty name-brand fifths from generic gallon containers. Finally, a slightly overweight woman in her early forties entered the joint and made her way toward Ricken-bacher. She hefted herself onto the stool next to him and ordered Jack Black straight up in a frozen shot glass, her sensuously low and throaty voice completely at odds with her appearance.

She had a temporary beauty, applied carefully each morning, then scrubbed off each night with Noxema and a cosmetic sponge. Beneath all the make-up existed one of the homeliest women Rickenbacher had ever met, but she could do things with her mouth and her tongue that most men couldn't even imagine until she did it to them for twenty bucks. Colette had semi-retired from the street and made most of her living describing sexual intercourse to lonely men who dialed a 900 number and paid $2.50 a minute to masturbate to the sound of her voice. A hooker with a heart of gold is a fiction perpetuated by television cop shows, but Colette was the next best thing.

She owed Rickenbacher a favor.

Rickenbacher pushed the slim file folder toward Colette. She lifted the cover and carefully examined a series of grainy black-and-white contact proofs. Two of them had been circled with orange grease pencil, and Colette's eight-year-old niece, her thin lips wrapped around the fat head of a rubber dildo, stared up at her from each of them. Then Colette thumbed through the strips of 35mm negatives used to create the proofs, assuring herself that all were accounted for. When she finally closed the cover, Colette griped the folder so tightly it began to crumple and her knuckles turned white.

When her drink arrived a moment later, Colette wrapped one handful of ring-encrusted fingers around the sweating glass. Before she lifted it to her lips, she said, "I saw this morning's paper."

"Yeah?"

"Poor Mr. Johnson did a nose dive into the sidewalk outside his office." Colette lifted the shot glass to her heavily-painted red mouth, pressed the rim against the poorly-camouflaged cold sore on her bottom lip, and tilted her head backward as she lifted the glass upward. The auburn liquid disappeared down the back of her throat. When she finished, she said, "I figure I have you to thank for that."

"He tripped."

Colette turned to consider Rickenbacher. The brim of his baseball cap shadowed Rickenbacher's eyes and she could read nothing in them. He slid a copy of Katherine Cove's high school graduation photo from his shirt pocket and laid it face-up in front of Colette.

Carlos eased down the bar with a bottle in one hand and tried to refill Colette's shot glass while she stared at the young woman's face. She waved him away. "One's enough, honey."

"Ever seen her?" Rickenbacher asked.

"Seen dozens like her," Colette said. "They come and they go. They just don't come too often in my neighborhood." She laughed at her own joke, but the sound disappeared when she realized she laughed alone. "Haven't seen her."

Rickenbacher slid the photo down the bar toward Carlos. "You?"

Carlos shook his head.

Rickenbacher told them both, "You do, you'll let me know."

"Honey, come up to my place some night and I'll give you something you'll never get from some young pussy." She smiled.

Rickenbacher pushed himself off the stool and towered above Colette for the moment it took him to adjust his baseball cap securely over his bald spot. Then he headed toward the door.

"Hey, Big Dick," Colette called to his back. "You know how I'm gonna die? Hearing aids!" she shouted. "From all you pricks who think oral sex means talking about it."

Carlos stood behind the bar laughing quietly. He refilled Colette's glass with imitation Jack and told her the drink was on the house. She watched Rickenbacher until he stepped through the door, then she upended her drink on the file folder. She reached into her purse for a disposable lighter, flicked it to life, and held the flame to the corner of the folder.

"Jesus, lady!" Carlos swore as he swatted at the burning folder with his bar towel. "You trying to burn the place down?"

The folder, the contact proofs, and the negatives had turned to ash and melted plastic before the bartender put the fire out. He managed to save only the photo of Katherine Cove, and he slid it under the cash register.

Rickenbacher had never actually cruised the information highway himself. Instead, he traveled the back alleys and side streets, where information cost him a five spot, a drink, or a favor, and he wore out more shoe leather than RAM. Throughout the day, he reached out to people who might have seen Katherine if she had fallen from grace, and made connections with people who just hung around keeping their eyes open. Unlike the big agency Cove had initially hired, Rickenbacher preferred to do the work personally, ensuring that every base was covered, every angle considered, every resource used.

After he left Colette at the Muff Inn, Rickenbacher dropped five spots and sprang for drinks at a dozen different clubs, strip joints, and newsstands. Some days were better than others and when he finally stopped for dinner at a fast-food joint serving greasy burgers and greasier fries, he knew no more than he'd known that morning.

The sun had already slid down the evening sky leaving a trail of tainted smog when Lieutenant Castellano reviewed the preliminary reports. Uniforms had canvassed the neighborhood where Jane Doe 43 had died, interviewing bartenders and bouncers, hookers and housewives, winos and waitresses, and had come up with nothing. No one knew who she was or how she came to die in a cheap hotel room.

He hadn't seen Jane Doe 43's face on any milk cartons, nor on any missing persons reports. He stood before a battered grey cabinet and thumbed through the files, looking for any indication that someone missed her and wanted her to return. Later, he phoned the country's three largest private organizations devoted to the location of missing children, his hopes of successfully identifying her diminishing with each call until he finally gave up.

His shift ended before his patience gave out, but when it did, he sat at his desk fingering the silver locket he wore on a chain under his starched white shirt. He had a splitting headache and he wanted a beer.

Maybe more than one.

Paul Canfield stood in the back, behind the runway stage near the door to the men's room. Above him a neon Budweiser sign popped and fizzled as it tried repeatedly to burn itself out. He watched the anemic redhead on stage bump and grind without sincerity until the men's room door finally opened and a corpulent salesman in an off-the-rack suit that hadn't fit properly in years came waddling out, followed closely by the scent of flatulence, stale sperm, and cheap cologne. Canfield coughed into his fist, then pushed his way into the tiny room and locked the door.

He pressed down the handle on the faucet and a thin trickle of tepid water flowed over his hands. Canfield splashed the water on his face, then threaded his damp fingers through his hair and pushed the long locks of black and grey away from his forehead. After a moment, he tried to focus on his reflection in the mirror, but the dim light from the 40-watt bulb above him and the graffiti carved into the polished-steel sheet nailed to the wall over the sink prevented him from seeing anything more than the deep bags under his eyes. He hadn't slept since the previous morning.

Canfield wiped the front of the sink dry with his forearm, then reached into his shirt pocket and retrieved a glass vial. He shook a small pile of cocaine from the vial onto the sink, then used the switchblade he kept in his left boot to push the drug into a thin white line along the edge of the porcelain. He leaned forward, pressed his left nostril shut with his index finger, and then inhaled the entire line.

It took a moment for his body to react to the drug and before it did someone pounded on the door. "You buy that real estate, bud?"

After dinner, Rickenbacher cruised the stretch, stopping to talk to every young blonde hooker parading her wares, finally returning home alone that evening. Mrs. Stegmann's annoying white poodle stood on the back of her overstuffed couch and barked at him through the window as he slowly made his way up the stairs to his apartment. As soon as he slipped his key into the lock and twisted, Rickenbacher realized he had company. He pushed the door open slowly, prepared for most anything. He'd had unexpected visitors before — too many times before — and they weren't often friendly.

Lieutenant Castellano sat on Rickenbacher's couch, thumbing through a two-week old *TV Guide*. A six-pack of Budweiser, four cans still captured in the plastic-ring carrier, sat on the floor beside the couch. The Lieutenant had already finished one beer and he held a second in his left hand. Without looking up at Rickenbacher, he said, "Didn't figure I needed a warrant."

Rickenbacher relaxed as he closed the door.

"Seems your friend really did trip." Castellano closed the magazine he'd been glancing through and tossed it to the other end of the couch. "We found some loose carpeting near his desk."

Rickenbacher nodded. There hadn't been any loose carpeting in Mr. Johnson's office when he'd left.

"The Medical Examiner confirmed cause of death as a broken neck, but it looks like Johnson ran into something before he fell. The M.E. said Johnson landed on his back, but his nose had been broken before the fall."

"Maybe he ran into a door."

"Stranger things have happened," the Lieutenant said. "Somebody clumsy enough to fall out a window could have run into a door first."

Rickenbacher just shrugged his shoulders.

Castellano said, "We found a few other things as well."

"Yeah?"

"Three file cabinets filled with photos of young girls. One of the drawers had been opened and rifled." Castellano sat silent for a moment, then asked, "How's your hand?"

"Healing nicely."

The Lieutenant lifted the Budweiser can to his lips and drained it. The last time he'd been in Rickenbacher's apartment he'd put away a six of Bud and a fifth of Jack and had spent half the night driving the porcelain bus, heaving his guts out. He asked, "You working on anything these days?"

"Missing girl." Rickenbacher tossed the folder on his coffee table. Missing girls had become his specialty.

Castellano reached down for another beer, popped it open, then reached for the folder. He opened it and spent a moment staring at Katherine Cove. "Looks like another small town dreamer. She come to the big city to find her fortune?"

"Don't know why she came," Rickenbacher answered. He peeled off his windbreaker and his baseball cap and stuffed them in his coat closet. Then he glanced at his answering machine and found no messages waiting. He said, "Not even sure she made it here."

"Mommy want her little girl to come home?"

"Daddy does."

"I got a girl just like her on ice. She's tore up so bad you can't tell what she looked like. Got a few good prints off her left hand, but there's no match."

Rickenbacher didn't say anything.

"*Dragnet*'s on in fifteen minutes," Castellano said. "Let's watch something with a happy ending."

"You need a wife to go home to," Rickenbacher said. His former partner had never married. "Then you wouldn't need to hang around here."

"When did you become an authority on marriage?"

Rickenbacher shrugged. He found an unopened bag of pretzels in the kitchen, poured himself a large glass of unsweetened orange juice, and then sat on the couch beside his former partner. They watched old programs on Rickenbacher's portable black-and-white television until Castellano finished the last beer, pissed, and went home.

The woman on stage at the Muff Inn had been flatchested until her twenty-second birthday when a plastic surgeon who'd received his medical degree from a disreputable Mexican university had stretched the skin on her chest taut across a pair of silicon bags. The make-up she used to hide the scars under her cosmetically-inflated breasts and below her pale pink nipples ran in sweaty rivulets down her abdomen to catch in the thick mat of curly black pubic hair at the junction of her thighs. The men in the audience didn't seem to mind that the breasts jutting from her chest didn't move naturally, nor did they care that the thin caesarean bikini-cut scar along the top of her pubic hair continued to remind her of the still-born daughter she'd had while a high school sophomore. Those who could still focus their eyes after an evening of drinking three dollar beers cared only that she might spread her legs for them in the privacy of a back room if they offered her enough money.

Canfield knew better. The raven-haired bitch on stage had been working the crowd between shows for months, but had never done more than a few quick hand jobs under the tables, pleasuring the lonely while whispering dirty words in their ears. It was a service he'd never requested.

He slapped a crumpled five on the bar and Carlos quickly replaced it with a cold bottle of Busch. "Last call, Mr. Canfield. You want I should open another bottle for you?"

Canfield shook his head. A line of coke with a half-dozen beer chasers had taken him just where he'd wanted to go.

He watched as the woman on stage spun her g-string around on her index finger, then let it fly into the audience. An inebriated Marine who looked young enough to have lied about his age to the recruiting officer, caught it and brought it to his face. His three older buddies laughed and hollered as he took a deep whiff of the dancer's scent. Then she looked straight at him and licked her glossy red lips with the tip of her tongue, a seductive gesture that Canfield knew was just part of the show.

"She wants you, Eddie!" the Marine's buddies shouted. They pushed him to his feet as the dancer made her way off stage and the music ended.

"Didn't you see her?"

"She wants you, man."

"Go back stage and slip her the pork, Eddie. You know she wants it."

Goaded by his friends, the young Marine headed toward the dressing rooms in back. Carlos reached under the bar and flipped a switch. A red light flashed in the back hallway and Ben Kirkland, a squat fireplug of a man who stood just about as wide as he stood tall, prepared to meet the unwanted guest.

Canfield laughed a few minutes later when the young Marine returned, his uniform torn and his face bloodied.

"She didn't want me, man. She didn't want nobody," he explained.

"Who the fuck did this to you?"

"She got a boyfriend back there? A bouncer?" The Marines stood, ready to extract revenge for their buddy's blood.

"No man, there's three or four of them back there. Don't start nothing, man. Let's just get the hell out of here."

"What've you got planned tonight, Mr. Canfield?" Carlos asked as the Marines headed for the door. He knew all about Canfield's predilection for underage girls. "Anything special?"

Canfield shook his head. "Not tonight. You?"

Carlos smiled. One of the new dancers had promised him head if he scored a little blow for her. Blow for a blow. "Could be, Mr. Canfield. Could be."

Chapter 4

Rickenbacher woke with dreams of his second wife still fresh in his mind. She'd been a slim blonde eight years his junior, eager and uninhibited in the bedroom, but the marriage had dissolved within a year and she'd moved to Scottsdale to live with an effete painter who dabbed colors on canvas and called it art. He often dreamed of the women in his life — Agnes, Jesse, Sandy, and the others — the dreams blending together until he could no longer recall who was who and who had done what to whom. After a moment's hesitation, Rickenbacher flipped the sheet back, climbed out of bed, and made his way to the bathroom, where he stood before the toilet and stared down at the stain ringing the inside of the bowl. It took longer than usual for his erection to subside, despite his best efforts to imagine anything other than his ex-wife.

The phone rang and continued to ring until he padded

his way back into the bedroom and picked up the handset. He pressed it to his ear and said, "Rickenbacher."

Colette said, "I've been thinking about your question."

"Yeah?"

"You talk to Bleach yet?" she asked, her voice reminding him why she could make a living talking lonely men into self-induced orgasm. "He gets all the fresh ones."

"Where's he spend his time?"

"Fifth and Armitage." She described the mulatto pimp's appearance. "You can't miss him."

Lieutenant Castellano sat in his office, rearranging the poorly-typed reports from the Mobile Crime Scene officers and the computer-generated reports from the Medical Examiner and the Crime Lab. He'd been through the case file more than a dozen times and he knew little more than he had known before he'd opened the manila folder. The young girl he'd seen dissected in a cheap motel room the previous day still had no name. She remained Jane Doe 43.

On the far left corner of his desk were two photos, each captured within its own polished silver frame, and they caught the Lieutenant's gaze as he flipped over a report from the first officer on the scene. The newest photo featured his parents at their 50th wedding anniversary; the oldest was his sister Maria's seventh grade class picture. She'd been a contraceptive miscalculation, born two months after Castellano joined the Marines and four years before he entered the Police Academy, to parents who had already set their sights on retirement. The photographer's studio had delivered the plastic-wrapped set of eight-by-tens, five-by-sevens, and two-dozen wallet-sized glossies a week after her mutilated body had been found in a drainage ditch three miles from the junior high school. He and Rickenbacher had closed the case some years later, pinning the rap on a serial killer.

The Lieutenant rested his right elbow on the top of his highly-polished desk, then leaned forward and caught the bridge of his nose between his thumb and his middle finger. He squeezed hard, trying to drive away the pounding at the back of his skull.

After five minutes of staring at his sister's photo — at her slender shoulders, her long black hair parted in the middle and pushed behind her ears, the locket that hung into the budding cleavage hinted at by her low-cut white blouse, the smile that pulled the corners of her lips apart just enough to reveal the dull silver wire of her retainer — a knock on his office door finally tore Castellano's attention in another direction. He straightened the reports and closed the file folder. Then he slid it into the top drawer of his desk and motioned for Sergeant Kowalski to enter his office. There were other cases to investigate and his attention had to be given to those the department might actually solve.

After Rickenbacher stepped from the shower, he leaned back over the tub and stuck his finger into the drain, retrieving a wad of freshly deposited hair. He snorted in disgust and flicked the soggy hairball toward a small plastic trash can wedged between the toilet bowl and the sink. It struck the wall and clung there like a crushed spider. His hair seemed to be abandoning him at an ever faster clip and he wondered how much longer he had until forced to part his hair at ear level and plaster long thin strands across the top of his cranium.

He toweled himself dry, brushed his wet hair straight back over the thinning spot on the crown of his head, then dressed. When he finally left the apartment, Rickenbacher wore faded blue jeans, a sleeveless grey sweatshirt, a pale blue windbreaker, and a baseball cap. He carried no weapons, relying instead on his size and his reputation to intimidate the people he dealt with.

Mrs. Stegmann pulled back one side of her heavy drapes and peered out at him when Rickenbacher's van coughed to life a few minutes later. Her pinched face had the shape and texture of an albino prune, but she allowed a tiny smile to tug at the corners of her mouth when she saw Rickenbacher. He gave her a half-salute before reaching down to the stick shift and dropping the van into gear.

Although they rarely spoke, she collected his mail whenever he was away for more than two days, and every Christmas she baked him three dozen chocolate chip cookies. In return, Rickenbacher had let the neighborhood acne-and-crack crowd know that messing with Mrs. Stegmann or her irritating poodle was the same as messing with him.

If brains were breasts, the woman in the bed beside Paul Canfield wouldn't have had enough for cleavage. He'd married her four years earlier and she still had no idea how he earned a living, even though she told all her friends he was in sales. She couldn't cook, so she prepared a lot of microwave meals, and she couldn't clean, so Canfield paid an illegal immigrant to come in once a week. He paid his wife's annual membership at the health club and her monthly bill at the tanning salon. In return, she kept him up-to-date on Oprah and Jerry Springer and all the characters on *General Hospital*, an arrangement they had not anticipated when they'd stood before the Elvis impersonator in Las Vegas four years earlier, but one they'd both come to accept.

She rolled onto her back and her heavy breasts slid toward each armpit. Four years earlier he might have pushed the sheet back and buried his face between her thighs, bringing her awake with his tongue. Even two years previously, he might have leaned forward and taken one of her thick nipples between his teeth, nipping at it to see if she

roused. Now, Canfield just glanced at her to assure himself
that her sudden movement wasn't a precursor to awakening.
He didn't feel like explaining why he wouldn't be able to get
an erection when he was with her and he didn't feel like
discussing why the household budget for vibrator batteries
had recently quadrupled.

Canfield slid out of bed, careful not to disturb his wife,
and padded across the bedroom to the chair where he'd
thrown his clothes the night before. He pulled on his jeans
before he left the bedroom and he padded through the house
barefoot, finding the baggie he'd stashed earlier in the week
tucked under the box spring in the guest bedroom.

He did a line of coke in the guest bathroom and as soon
as it hit, he knew it would be a good day. Perhaps he'd even
find Bleach and spend some time with one of his other girls.

Before then, he had to make an appointment because
money didn't grow on trees. He picked up the phone and
punched in Walston's number at the Fuzzy Clam.

K atherine Cove had woven herself into the fabric of
the city without leaving any loose threads for Rickenbacher
to pick at. Without court orders and search warrants, some
avenues of exploration were denied to him, but old friends
and people who owed Rickenbacher favors had accessed a
number of corporate and government computer data bases
and had all managed to confirm what the others had already
discovered. However Katherine Cove earned a living, however she paid her bills, however she survived in Windy City,
if she was even in the city, it was without leaving a paper
trail.

He'd tried all of his usual sources and a few unusual
ones as well, and if he hadn't nearly run down Jesse two
nights earlier, he probably would not have thought to ask for
her help. He'd never tried to track people through their

library cards and she was the only librarian he knew.

The drive from Rickenbacher's apartment to the main branch of the library took less than half an hour in early morning traffic. He parked on the street, dropped a pair of quarters into the meter, and made his way up the thirty-seven marble steps between the two lions, and into the building. He hadn't been to the library in years and it took him two wrong turns and one request for assistance before he finally made his way to the children's section.

She saw him first.

"Jesus," Jesse Kegel said under her breath. She reached up and touched her hair, unconsciously pushing a few wild wisps back into place.

Rickenbacher saw her then, sitting on the hardwood floor surrounded by nearly a dozen toddlers, a picture book in her hand. The last time he'd seen her prior to nearly running her down with his van, she'd been wearing a cap and gown and carrying a degree in library sciences. She hadn't seen him then because he hadn't wanted her to. He'd found a seat in the rear of the auditorium and had slipped out after she'd received her diploma.

Jesse pushed herself off the floor and smoothed her pleated skirt against her thighs. Her dishwater blonde hair had become threaded with grey since the last time they'd seen one another and tiny crow's feet now adorned the corners of her emerald green eyes. She'd gained weight over the years, mostly in the rear, and her breasts needed under-wire support to maintain the false perkiness they'd once had naturally. Rickenbacher didn't notice the changes. He saw instead the young waitress from Doughnut World he'd flirted with for almost three months before she took him back to her apartment on the university campus where she had just begun her sophomore year.

That first time she'd danced the mattress mambo like a virgin who'd seen too many porno movies; she had the moves, but no agility and no grace, and when he finally penetrated her, she was almost painfully tight. Their relationship had lasted nearly six months before his first wife forced him to end it.

They drifted apart, not crossing paths until years later, after Rickenbacher had been promoted to Vice and she'd stuck her head in his unmarked car while he was trolling for prostitutes. He had recognized her despite her painfully thin body, the glazed look in her eyes, and the thick layer of make-up hiding the bruises on her face and neck. It had been a long, hard fall from college to the gutter and she spent the rest of the night telling him about it over an endless supply of bad coffee. The next day her pimp was busted with 12 grams of coke he claimed had been planted on him, and Jesse had disappeared from the street. With a cash stake that nearly eliminated Rickenbacher's retirement fund, Jesse returned to college.

"It's been a long time." Jesse wet her lips with the tip of her tongue, then asked, "How've you been?"

"The same."

"Still a cop?"

He shook his head and she looked him a question. He said, "I had a disagreement with Internal Affairs."

A tow-headed boy tugged at Jesse's skirt to claim her attention. He looked up at her, his pale blue eyes reflecting the fluorescent light in such a way that they seemed to twinkle, and he asked what happened to the glass slipper. Jesse caught one of the assistants and asked him to finish reading *Cinderella* to the toddlers. She explained to Rickenbacher, "Storytime twice a week. I usually read to them myself."

"You look good," he said as Jesse led him into her office, a room not much larger than a walk-in closet and overflowing with children's books, magazines, and grant applications. The walls were covered with crayon representations of fairy tale and nursery rhyme characters. Rickenbacher recognized Little Red Riding Hood and Jack Be Nimble but the others evaded his cognitive skills. On one corner of her badly scarred oak desk sat a computer terminal covered with Post-It notes.

As she closed the door behind them, Jesse asked, "So what does an ex-cop do?"

There were only two chairs in the room, and Jesse took the one behind the desk. Rickenbacher wedged himself into the other one, pushed it back against the wall and pressed his knees against the front of her desk.

"I look for . . . people."

"A private eye?"

He shook his head. "Can't get a license. Not sure I want one."

The gleam in Jesse's eyes faded. "You're working now, aren't you?"

"Yeah."

Guardedly, she asked, "What do you think I can do for you?"

Rickenbacher explained about Katherine Cove and how she'd disappeared. "She was a smart kid, good grades, a voracious reader. I need to know if she's got a library card."

"I can only access the city system," Jesse explained as she turned to the computer and entered the missing girl's name. "If she's got a library card anywhere in the suburbs, it won't show up here."

"How can I find out?" Rickenbacher asked.

"One suburb at a time," Jesse suggested. The computer beeped and she looked down at the screen. "Nothing here. I've got a Eudella Cove and a Kenny Cove, but no Katherine."

Rickenbacher copied the addresses into his notebook, just in case.

"Anything else?" Jesse asked. When Rickenbacher hesitated, she said, "If not, I have to get back out there with the kids."

She stood, then he stood. Jesse tried to step past him to the door, but Rickenbacher gathered her into his arms, cupped a hand under her chin and tilted her face upward. She didn't resist when he leaned over and covered her mouth with his. Her lips were soft and full, and they parted to allow their tongues to begin a fiery dance inside her mouth.

When he finally pulled away, Jesse struggled to catch her breath. Her face had flushed and her eyelids fluttered. She said, "It's been a long time."

"Too long."

"A lot of water under the bridge."

"Is there anybody in your life?"

"Not even a cat."

One of the assistants called Jesse's name and she told Rickenbacher, "I have to get back out there." She waved one hand vaguely at the door. "I can't . . . Jesus, Rickenbacher, you turn up like a bad penny every time I think I'm over you." The assistant called Jesse's name again. She opened the door and stepped into the hall. She didn't look back when she said, "My number's in the book. It's always been in the book."

He watched her hips sway as she walked away and he waited until she'd disappeared into the children's department before he made his way toward the main exit two floors up.

Rickenbacher had a number of places to visit after he left the library and he scanned the list he'd jotted in his notebook to determine the most efficient route.

"Got any smokes?" Lieutenant Castellano asked a few hours later when they both sat in the Lieutenant's office.

"I thought you quit." Rickenbacher reached into his jacket pocket and retrieved a crumpled pack of generic menthols and a half-used book of matches from the Muff Inn. He tossed them on the Lieutenant's desk. They slid halfway across.

"More than once." Castellano shook a bent cigarette loose from the pack and repeatedly straightened it with his slender fingers. While he stroked the cigarette, the Lieutenant stared over Rickenbacher's left shoulder at a pale white hooker whose face looked like it had been hit hard with the flat side of a shovel. A uniform pushed her into a dented metal folding chair and she sat with her knobby knees pressed together and her feet splayed apart. A vacant glaze settled over her eyes.

"Gonna smoke it, or wait till it cums in your hand?" Rickenbacher asked. He'd visited admissions at three local universities and a junior college before coming to his former partner's office to search the department's booking sheets for Katherine Cove's name and to check the homicide records for mention of a teenaged blonde. He'd done the same thing a few days earlier, but after ten minutes, the computer still drew a blank.

Lieutenant Castellano trapped the cigarette between his index finger and his middle finger and lifted it toward his lips. His slim hand stopped in mid-air. "Aren't we looking for the same thing?"

"What's that?"

Something crashed in the squad room outside the Lieutenant's office and a coarse baritone blasphemed the Lord three different ways before the commotion finally settled. Rickenbacher and Castellano had spent too many years inside squad rooms to be startled by anything less than gunfire. Their conversation continued unabated.

"A young girl."

"Yeah?"

"The difference is, mine's dead. Jane Doe 43. I want to know who she is." Castellano finally captured the cigarette between his lips and reached for the black-and-gold match-book. He flipped it open, tore out a paper match, carefully closed the cover, then snapped the match to life. He held the flame against the end of his cigarette and inhaled. After lighting the cigarette, he snuffed the flame out with the thumb and forefinger of his left hand, then tossed the dead match into a glass ashtray that had been as clean as his desk.

"I talked to Gilly Boy Thomas about it," he said after a few deep drags on the cigarette.

"He's out?"

"About six months now. He rolled over on his cousin and copped a lesser. Time off for good behavior." The District Attorney's office hadn't had enough to convict either cousin for the murder of a 36-year-old stockbroker they'd caught jogging in the park after sundown until Gilly Boy mentioned a peanut-shaped birthmark on the woman's left breast. His attorney realized what Gilly Boy had said and immediately taught him the art of self-preservation. Gilly Boy metaphorically stuck a knife in his cousin's back just as surely as one of them had stuck a knife between the stockbroker's third and fourth ribs. "Said he didn't know a thing about it, but asked if he could keep the photographs I showed him."

"Fingerprints?"

"Hundreds. Hell," Castellano said, "even one of mine. If I managed that hotel, I'd fire the maids." He took a long draw from the cigarette, held the smoke in for a moment, then released it through his nostrils. "The blood's all hers, but he left semen in every orifice."

"And?"

"He's not a secretor." They both knew that body-type antigens are found in the body fluids of a secretor and that testing a secretor's sweat, saliva, or semen reveals their blood type. "We've got nothing."

The Lieutenant pulled a slim manila folder from the top

drawer of his desk and slid it across to Rickenbacher. The big man read the reports and examined the photos. He said, "People die in that neighborhood every day. Why the personal interest?"

Castellano took one last draw from the cigarette, then tamped it out in the ashtray. A single ash blew onto his desktop, but he didn't notice. "She couldn't have been more than sixteen or seventeen when she walked into that room. She'd never done anything like that before."

"Yeah?"

"The girl's hymen had been torn. She almost died a virgin."

Rickenbacher knew the routine. The girl had no name, she hadn't been reported to the Missing Persons Bureau, there were no suspects, and the city had cut the department's budget during a year when only three more homicides would set a new record. If it weren't for the Lieutenant's personal interest, the girl's case file would have already been buried in a cabinet somewhere in the basement.

"If I hear anything, I'll pass it along." As Rickenbacher stood to leave, he noticed oily fingerprints smudging the silver frame around Castellano's sister's photo, dulling the finish. The Lieutenant always kept the two frames polished and seeing prints only on the one frame helped Rickenbacher better understand Castellano's interest in Jane Doe 43. It was the same reason Rickenbacher specialized in searching for missing girls. The big man wrapped his fist around the door knob, but before he could turn it, Castellano spoke his name.

He turned. "Yeah?"

"Your smokes." The Lieutenant used his forefinger to push the battered pack back across the desk toward his former partner.

"Keep the pack," Rickenbacher said. "You need them worse than I do."

As the Lieutenant spotted the single cigarette ash on his desktop and carefully brushed it into his open palm, Rickenbacher stepped from Castellano's meticulously organized office into the kaleidoscopic reality of the squad room, where the only way to tell the good guys from the bad was by the amount of paperwork with which they had to contend.

Chapter 5

Wounded skies streaked with bloody clouds opened up and pelted Rickenbacher with hard-driven rain as he made his way along the three-block long stretch of strip joints and pornographic book stores. The barkers stepped back into open doorways, their cries muted by the rain.

Near the north end of the third block, sandwiched between Peepers and XXX Books and Tapes, a coffee shop named Good Eats had survived the ups and downs of the neighborhood around it, and Rickenbacher ducked inside. Despite the torrential rain, Good Eats remained nearly deserted, save for a bag lady mumbling into a glass of water in a booth near the back and a nervous young man with orange spiked hair who kept looking over his shoulders as if expecting company. Unlike most of the businesses on the stretch, the interior of Good Eats bathed in fluorescent light, the chrome and white Formica gleaming despite years of abuse.

Rickenbacher shook the rain off his jacket and his base-ball cap before striding the length of the counter. He swung his leg over the last stool and motioned for the waitress. He hadn't eaten since morning and didn't need to review the menu before ordering.

The lone waitress had spent most of her life working on the stretch, having once been a dancer in the clubs when a flash of thigh or a hint of breast remained sufficient to drive male patrons into a frenzy, long before full nudity became mandatory. Now she had her silver hair piled into a beehive and held in place by a paper cap, wore a food-stained white uniform stretched taut at the hips, and white Reeboks that squeaked every time she stopped or turned. She took Rick-enbacher's order without emotion, then called it out to the sweating Greek behind the grill.

"Adam and Eve on a raft. Wreck 'em," she yelled as she poured coffee thick as motor oil into a chipped white mug. She slid it across the counter to Rickenbacher and he held his hands over the steaming mug to warm them.

Rickenbacher had consumed half of his scrambled eggs on toast and had started on his second cup of coffee when the door opened and a squat fireplug of a man stepped in out of the rain. He wore faded Levi's held up by a thick black leather belt and a large silver Harley-Davidson buckle fas-tened low under his ample gut. A royal blue tank-top re-vealed the bulging muscles of his shoulders and upper arms. His body was the canvas upon which the Michelangelos of tattoo had etched their masterpieces, and nearly every inch of his skin had been covered with ink. When he saw Rick-enbacher at the far end of the counter, he smiled.

Ben Kirkland swaggered the length of the counter, then hiked himself up on the stool next to the big man. His solution to male pattern baldness had been to completely shave his skull to reveal the dragons, daggers, and damsels someone had etched into the skin of his head. Fluorescent light reflected off the beaded water on Ben's head and into Rickenbacher's eyes.

"Heard what you did to Johnson," Ben said.

"He tripped."

Ben snorted, the sound remarkably close to that of a Razorback with congestion. "And that makes me the Queen of San Francisco."

Rickenbacher shrugged, then lifted another forkful of tightly scrambled eggs to his mouth. As the big man chewed, the waitress squeaked over and Ben ordered a third-pound burger, rare with onions.

"There's a few people upset about what happened to Johnson," Ben continued.

"You one of them?"

"Johnson deserved what he got."

Rickenbacher finished his eggs and toast, then shook a cigarette out of a fresh pack he'd retrieved from the glove compartment of his van. As he lifted it to his lips, the waitress hurriedly squeaked over.

"Hey buddy," she said. "This here's the no smoking section."

Rickenbacher glanced around the coffee shop but didn't see any ashtrays. "Where's — ?"

She interrupted before he could finish the question. "Outside, if you gotta smoke."

Rickenbacher captured the unlit cigarette between his lips and asked his smaller companion, "You still at the Muff Inn?"

"Most nights," Ben said. "I fill in for a guy over at Aphrodite's a couple times a month."

Rickenbacher pulled a copy of Katherine Cove's graduation photo from his pocket. "You seen her around, looking for work?"

"We don't mess with jailbait."

"She's legal, barely."

"Haven't seen her, but I can keep my eyes open."

Rickenbacher sucked on the unlit cigarette, but felt no satisfaction. He watched the bag lady shuffle out the door when the rain stopped and she disappeared around the corner. When Ben's burger arrived a moment later, Rickenbacher excused himself, dropped a battered five on the counter, and left.

He had already cruised through most of the strip joints and flop houses but he still had many places to visit in the neighborhood, places to flash Katherine's photo and hope for a response.

Happy's Books, around the corner and a block away from the three-block stretch containing most of the clubs and the bookstores, had a large selection of used books in the front room and an equally large selection of pornographic magazines in the back. Elmer Hapgood, once the proprietor of a clean, well-lit bookstore safe for patrons of all ages, had nearly given up all hope of making his living from literature.

Hapgood shook like a quarter-bed in a cheap hotel, his palsy particularly bad this day. Rickenbacher placed Katherine Cove's photo on the counter next to the cash register and asked the old man to look at it.

Hapgood leaned forward on his stool, adjusted his bifocals, and squinted at the picture.

"Ever seen her before?"

Hapgood looked up at Rickenbacher. "What's she done?"

"Runaway. I'm looking for her."

"What'd she run from?"

"Don't think she was running from as much as she was running to."

"To what?"

"Bright lights, big city."

The palsied old man considered Rickenbacher's answer,

then said, "I think she's been in a few times. She's changed her hair, cut it short like that skater, Dorothy Hamill, and she's lost weight, gotten rid of that baby fat."

"You sure it's her?"

"Hell, I ain't sure I had a bowel movement this morning. I just think I seen her in here a few times."

"Know where she lives?"

"Must be close by." Hapgood shrugged. "Nobody comes here for the paperbacks unless they live close by."

"When she leaves here, which way does she go?"

"Sometimes she goes left, sometimes she goes right. I ain't in the habit of paying all that much attention."

Rickenbacher placed one of his business cards on the counter, a five folded underneath it. "She comes in again, give me a call."

"Not much is it?" said the officer standing on the far side of the counter. Murphey had been in charge of the evidence locker ever since a lead pipe had damaged the cartilage in his knee bad enough to keep him from walking a beat, but not bad enough for a medical discharge.

Lieutenant Castellano stared into the box containing Jane Doe 43's clothing. He looked down at the blood-red tube top, black leather mini-skirt, sheer black pantyhose, and one red spike-heel pump, each item carefully bagged and tagged. "Where's her other shoe?"

"Check the report," said Murphey. He scratched at his bulbous nose as he spoke. "The officers on the scene didn't recover it."

"It didn't walk off by itself. Where'd it go?"

Murphey shrugged. "I wasn't there Lieutenant. I can't help you."

Castellano looked up at him for the first time in many minutes. "No, I guess you can't."

"You going to sign this stuff out, Lieutenant, or can I put it away?"

Castellano shook his head slowly, then pushed the box across the counter. He'd seen what he needed to see. Somebody would go down for the murder, but nothing in the box could help him locate a suitable suspect.

There were seven Coves listed in the city's telephone directory, including Kenny, and Rickenbacher had contacted all of them earlier in the week. Eudella Cove had an unlisted number, so he drove to the address she'd listed on her library card application and found himself parked in the driveway of a small, well-maintained bungalow.

Rickenbacher made his way from his van to the front steps of the house under the watchful eyes of most of the neighbors. Before he even reached out to ring the bell, a middle-aged man the color and shape of a bowling pin called out to him from the sidewalk.

"What do you want with Eudella?"

Rickenbacher turned and looked down the steps as the other man waddled up the walk. "I'm looking for a girl who might be related to her."

"Eudella's not one for company. Did you call ahead?"

"I couldn't. Her number's not listed."

"That's right. It ain't."

The door opened behind Rickenbacher and he turned again. A slender black woman within kissing distance of 60 peered up at him through the closed screen door.

"You ever seen this man before, Eudella?" The human bowling pin joined Rickenbacher on the porch.

"No, sir, I can't say that I have."

Rickenbacher introduced himself, then explained the reason for his visit. By then, Eudella had unlatched the screen and she took the photo Rickenbacher offered, squinting at it because she'd left her reading glasses on the table next to her favorite chair.

A moment later she handed Katherine Cove's graduation photo to the other man on the porch. "Gerald, does this look like anyone I could be related to?"

He stifled a laugh. "No, ma'am, it doesn't."

"There anything else I can help you with, Mr. Rickenbacher?" she asked.

He shook his head, then left, convinced that Katherine Cove and Eudella Cove were not related.

K at lay on her bed, a second-hand romance novel captured in one hand, and she sighed when the story's dashing hero swept the innocent heroine off her feet and planted a heart-melting kiss on her soft, pliant lips. Before long she'd have to mark her page, close the book, and prepare for work.

Kat worked for cash — $2 for each item delivered, plus whatever she picked up in tips. Some nights she sat at the office with the rest of the company's second shift delivery crew watching old science fiction movies on one of the city's independent UHF stations. Other nights she raked in as much as $200, mostly from tips. Delivering small packages by bicycle wasn't the glamorous job she'd expected to find when she'd moved to the city, but it paid the rent on her efficiency apartment and allowed her to feed her addiction to paperback romances.

Sometimes the packages she delivered contained contracts and business reports too thick to FAX and not going far enough to FedEx. More often, the packages contained pornography, drugs, and other illicit material. Katherine knew none of this. She simply delivered each package as assigned, blissful in her ignorance and looking forward only to the solitary pleasure she enjoyed during her off-hours.

When she wasn't working, Kat lived between the pages

of the romances, knowing full well that she would never have a knight in shining armor come riding up on a white horse and sweep her off her feet.

The dancer had a rodent's face — jutting nose, small mouth, receding chin — and she used foundation like body putty to smooth her acne-scarred face, but the men in the audience didn't seem to notice. Instead they focused on the silver tassels she had fastened to her nipples. She spun them to the left, then she spun them to the right, then she spun the tassels in opposite directions.

A printing industries convention had filled the strip clubs along the stretch, including the Muff Inn where she performed. The men whistled, cheered, and applauded her one talent and the faster the rodent-faced brunette twirled the tassels on her breasts, the more they roared their approval.

The crowd kept Carlos hopping behind the bar and the owner had promised to call in another bartender to assist him. On the stage behind him, the dancer tired and lost her rhythm. First the left tassel stopped, then the right. She spun around, bent over, and shook her butt at the crowd. Then she straightened and hurried off stage just as the song ended.

Paul Canfield stepped out of the men's room as the rodent-faced brunette hurried off stage. He'd missed her act completely, but he hadn't really been paying attention to the strippers all night. He had a fresh load of coke up his nose and had begun to feel good again.

Bleach grabbed his arm and pulled him back into the shadows. He leaned close to Canfield's ear and, loud enough to be heard over the music when a stripper dressed as a cowgirl galloped onto the stage to a country-western tune, Bleach asked, "Where my girl?"

"I ain't no damn baby-sitter," Canfield said. He twisted

his arm out of Bleach's grasp.

"She didn't come back."

"Maybe she went home to her daddy," Canfield said. "How the fuck do I know?"

"You was the last one saw her."

"All the others came back, didn't they?"

"Not Nikki. Last time I see her, she with you."

On stage, the stripper wore only a ten-gallon hat and brown leather chaps. Her dark pubic hair glistened with sweat and sparkles, her breasts swayed in time to a driving country beat.

Ben Kirkland stepped from the shadows and encouraged the two arguing men to take their conversation out to the street. When Bleach finally stormed away, Canfield spat on the sidewalk. Under his breath, he muttered, "Damn nigger pimp."

Even as he swore, Canfield wondered who else would supply him with fresh fluff.

Gilly Boy Thomas sat in his mother's living room, staring at her withered husk. She sat on a dusty, overstuffed couch, holding a television remote control in one hand and her trifocals in the other hand. She wore a tattered pink bathrobe that could have wrapped twice around her frail body, and a food-stained cotton nightgown decorated with pale blue flowers. He still hadn't figured out how she'd lived so long and he couldn't wait for her to finally bite it.

"Sheryl did good, Mama," he said. "So did you."

His mother didn't respond. Instead, she settled her trifocals onto her face and began pressing a button on her television remote control, watching fragments of programs as they flipped past.

Gilly Boy pushed himself up from the lop-sided chair and shrugged into his overcoat. He had a pick-up to make for Walston. "I'm going out for awhile. You don't have to wait up."

His mother lifted her finger from the remote control, settling on a *Gilligan's Island* rerun. After Gilly Boy pulled the door shut behind him, she whispered curses under her breath.

J esse Kegel stared at the phone for a long time before lifting the receiver, but even after she'd brought it to her ear she couldn't force herself to dial Rickenbacher's number and she returned the receiver to its cradle in Mickey Mouse's hand. She lifted the receiver to her ear two more times before dialing a number.

It wasn't his.

Instead, she dialed the number for one of the libraries in the suburbs, explained who she was and what she wanted to the head librarian, made notes when she received the answer, and then worked her way through the other seven suburban libraries.

R ickenbacher found Bleach standing outside the Puss'n'boots and they exchanged cautious greetings.

"Why they call you Big Dick?"

Rickenbacher had received the nickname years before when he'd been a vice cop. A teenaged hooker who died in his arms had been the first to call him that to his face. He didn't mention this to the mulatto pimp who stood before him. Instead, Rickenbacher smiled around the cigarette that dangled from his thick lips and asked, "Why do you think?"

"You shittin' me. You just a white boy."

Rickenbacher took the cigarette from his mouth and flipped it into a pool of rainwater where the still-glowing cherry drowned with a soft hiss. Bleach had watched the burning cigarette arc away and now he returned his gaze to the taller man's face. Almost completely hidden under the shadow cast by the bill of his baseball cap, Rickenbacher's smile slowly faded. "I heard a rumor."

"Talk to me," Bleach said. "What you hear 'bout me?"

"You can provide certain —"

Bleach nervously shifted his weight from one foot to the other. He didn't like looking up at Rickenbacher.

"— kinds of private entertainment."

"AC/DC, half-and-half, around the world?" Bleach asked. "Blonde, brunette, skinhead?"

"Young."

"You wan' knock the fuzz off a peach?" Bleach asked.

"Maybe." Rickenbacher stood silent for a moment, as if imagining the deflowering of a teenaged girl.

Bleach shifted his weight again. It hadn't been a good day. One of his new girls had disappeared, he'd just had an argument with one of his best customers about it, and now an ex-cop stood in front of him asking for some baby bush.

Rickenbacher smiled slowly, then said, "I can pay."

"What you got in mind?"

Rickenbacher slipped the photo of Katherine Cove from his jacket pocket and handed it to Bleach. "I want her."

The mulatto pimp snorted. "I can get you pussy, bro', but you got to order from the menu."

"It's her or not at all."

Bleach tightened his focus on the photo. "How much?"

Rickenbacher mentioned a number.

Bleach smiled. "I find her, you be the first to know."

"Yeah. Be sure of it."

Chapter 6

At a quarter of two in the morning, Rickenbacher began cruising the homeless shelters and the women's shelters. He showed Katherine Cove's photo to every priest, every security guard, and every volunteer he encountered. Some examined the photo carefully before shaking their head, others refused to examine it at all.

"No girls here," said one. "Just men."

"We can't give out that information," said another.

By the time the morning sun bled over the horizon, Rickenbacher had visited every shelter of which he'd ever heard, and Father Delvecchio of The Ninth Street Station, mistaking him for one of their regular clientele, had even offered Rickenbacher a cot before he'd had a chance to view Katherine's photo.

Rickenbacher had left his card at each place he'd visited, had even left copies of Katherine's photo at some of them, but he had little expectation that his efforts would prove fruitful. Katherine Cove had been swallowed by the city and the longer it took him to locate her, the less likely it was that she'd be belched out alive. Frustrated, Rickenbacher fought early morning traffic on his way home and he made it up the stairs to his apartment without disturbing Mrs. Stegmann's poodle. The big man checked his answering machine on his way through the living room, then stripped off his clothes and left them in a heap on the floor as he fell into bed.

Four hours and twelve minutes later, Rickenbacher woke with a start. He rolled over on his back and stared at the water stain for a full minute before he realized that someone had been pounding on his door and that whoever stood outside his apartment hadn't stopped. He groaned as he rolled out of bed, then he sorted through all the dirty clothes scattered across his bedroom floor until he found a pair of grey sweatpants. He pulled them on and padded through his apartment.

"They hurt my Percival," Mrs. Stegmann said as soon as Rickenbacher pulled the door open. She held the porcine little dog in her arms, nearly smothering him against her tiny bosoms.

"Who?"

"Them boys that are always hanging out at the corner."

"What'd they do?"

"They kicked Percival. He didn't do nothing to them."

"Who kicked him?"

"The thin one, with the tattoo on his arm."

Rickenbacher scratched his groin.

"I was coming home from the grocery. Just me and Percival."

The phone rang behind him.

"I'll take care of it," Rickenbacher said.

Mrs. Stegmann stared into his eyes for a moment, then nodded, knowing that he would. "I appreciate it."

Mrs. Stegmann turned to leave. The phone continued ringing while Rickenbacher pushed the door shut, then crossed the room to pick it up.

"Yeah?"

"Dick. . . ?"

Rickenbacher recognized Jesse Kegel's voice and his tone softened. "I'm here."

"Yesterday after you came to see me —" She hesitated. "I did some checking on my own. I know a lot of the librarians in the 'burbs and I had them all check. Nobody's given a card to a Katherine Cove."

"You saved me a lot of shoe leather," he said. "Thanks."

"I did the right thing?"

"Sure. I appreciate it."

"You sure she's here?"

"No," Rickenbacher said. "I just know she bought a one-way bus ticket to the city and she hasn't been heard from since."

"Oh." Then Jesse asked, "Do you think she's —"

"I'm betting against it. So's her father."

They lapsed into silence that stretched wire-thin. They each wanted the conversation to continue, but neither knew what to say. Finally, Jesse said, "Well, I've kids to care for. You need anything else, you call me, okay?"

"Sure," Rickenbacher said. "Sure, I will. Thanks."

Jesse disconnected first, leaving Rickenbacher standing in his living room, his big hand gripping the telephone handset so tightly it threatened to break in half. He'd turned his life inside out for her twice before and felt as if it was happening again.

After he finally showered and dressed, Rickenbacher selected his fedora and a light jacket before heading out. He walked down the stairs and past his green van, across the building's parking lot to the sidewalk. He saw five boys standing at the corner — ranging in age from mid-teens to early twenties — and he walked toward them.

Two shared a joint, passing it back and forth between hits, and two of the others argued about a recent drive-by shooting that had taken place about three miles south of where they stood. The fifth and obviously oldest of the five boys leaned against the outside wall of a dry cleaner, scraping his fingernails clean with the point of a switchblade. He was thin and wore a sleeveless white t-shirt that revealed a crude tattoo of a dragon his left forearm.

They paid no attention to Rickenbacher as he approached.

One of the two boys sharing the joint had an unnatural bulge under his shirt at the small of his back, but none of the others appeared to be carrying. When he stopped, Rickenbacher kept his eye on the little guy with the gun in his belt, but he addressed the acne-pocked boy with the tattoo and the switchblade.

"Real men don't kick poodles."

"You talking to me, or did your mouth fart?" Acne-face asked. The other four boys laughed.

"I don't like to repeat myself," Rickenbacher said.

One of the boys who'd been arguing about the drive-by whispered, "That's Big Dick, man, don't fuck with him."

The older boy ignored the advice and pushed himself away from the wall. "Yeah, well I don't like old people tellin' me what to do in my 'hood. And you ain't big enough to tell me what to do."

The boy with the bulge at the small of his back dropped the still-burning joint to the cracked sidewalk. He reached behind himself as Acne-face lifted his blade to waist-level.

As the pot-smoker brought the pistol from under his shirt and leveled it at him, Rickenbacher drove his left elbow into the boy's face, grabbed the boy's wrist with his right hand, and wrested away the .22, surprised and yet relieved at how under-powered the neighborhood's only gang seemed to be.

By then Acne-face had rushed forward, the switchblade aimed at Rickenbacher's abdomen. Rickenbacher knocked the boy's arm away, and spun to the side as the boy's momentum carried him past.

The pot-smoker who'd been relieved of the .22 dropped to his ass on the sidewalk and buried his face in his hands, crying. The other three boys backed away, leaving Rickenbacher and Acne-face to fight it out alone.

The boy with the switchblade came at Rickenbacher again, but this time Rickenbacher caught his wrist, spun him around, and pulled the boy's arm up behind his back, forcing him to drop the knife. He kicked the boy's feet out from under him and followed him to the ground.

Rickenbacher grabbed a handful of the boy's greasy hair, then smashed his face hard against the concrete, shattering his nose. He pressed the barrel of the .22 against the base of his skull. "You kiss the ground that poodle walks on."

"Jesus!" screamed the boy. "You motherfucking — !"

Rickenbacher lifted the back of the boy's head and drove his face against the concrete a second time.

This time, Acne-face kissed the pavement.

Rickenbacher released his grip on the gang leader and stood. He pocketed the .22, then scooped up the switch-blade and pocketed it, too. After adjusting his fedora, he asked, "Do I need to repeat myself?"

"No, sir," burbled the boy on the ground.

Satisfied, Rickenbacher turned his back on the five boys and returned to his apartment. Once inside, he unloaded the .22, noticing for the first time that the serial number had been etched off, wrapped both the pistol and the switch-blade in an old undershirt, and placed both weapons in a shoebox he placed on the top shelf of his bedroom closet. He didn't often carry weapons, but he knew that someday the two he'd just obtained would prove useful.

When he finished, Rickenbacher headed for his van.

T he dancer on stage could not legally be a customer of the club where she stripped, could not sit at the bar and order a drink, and yet each night after work she drank herself into a stupor and fell into bed. She told her family back in

Iowa that she was a dancer.

Canfield watched her intently.

On the stool next to him sat Walston, nursing a C.C.-and-Seven and waiting for Canfield to make the appropriate move. Finally, Canfield slid a key across the bar. Walston picked it up, glanced at the locker number, then replaced it with an envelope containing ten crisp hundred dollar bills. The transaction went smoothly and quickly, and as soon as Walston finished his drink, he pushed himself up off the stool and returned to the Fuzzy Clam where he spent most of his free time. Later that evening, he would have Gilly Boy or one of his other associates pick up the stolen traveler's checks waiting in a locker at the bus stop.

Rickenbacher spent most of the morning convincing a former client to access the Internal Revenue Service's records, just to discover that Katherine Cove had never filed a tax return, and he spent the afternoon with another former client, a doctor who accessed information about Katherine through the Medical Information Bureau. She had no record of alcohol or drug dependency, had no psychiatric problems, and had no sexually transmitted diseases. She was also still covered under her father's medical insurance.

He stopped at the public library's main branch on his way home and found Jesse in her office staring intently at a grant application. He rapped softly on her open door and she looked up. A smile fought to gain control of her face and it won.

"You came back," she said. Her eyes sparkled.

"Didn't realize how much I missed you until I saw you the other day," Rickenbacher explained. "I needed your help. I thought that's all I needed."

"I'll be done in twenty minutes," Jesse said.

"We can go somewhere. Talk about things."

"I'd like that," she said.

They met on the front steps after Jesse signed out for the evening, had foot-long hot dogs, greasy fries, and giant pretzels for dinner, then sat in the park across the street from the library and talked. Jesse told Rickenbacher about her life since graduation and how she'd worked her way up at the library; he told her about his last years on the force and how he'd been taking cases unofficially ever since.

What they didn't talk about was the man she'd become engaged to following graduation, even though she'd ultimately broken the engagement when she'd discovered his collection of gay magazines, nor did they discuss Rickenbacher's short-lived second marriage.

When it grew dark, Rickenbacher offered to take Jesse home. She smiled, thanked him for the offer, and declined. She knew what had happened the previous times the paths of their lives had intersected and she didn't want it to happen again.

"

did okay, didn't I?"

"You did fine," Gilly Boy told his next-door neighbor. "Don't talk about it any more."

"I told them I saw you at home. That was good wasn't it?"

Gilly Boy backhanded Sheryl and her head snapped to the side. "I told you to shut up about it."

Sheryl tasted blood where an incisor had cut the inside of her lip when Gilly Boy hit her. She reached up and touched the corner of her mouth with one finger. "Don't I always do what you want me to do?"

He slapped her again. "I want you to shut up!"

"But, Gilly —"

He grabbed her arm and slammed her face-forward into the dining room wall. An aging wedding photo of a now-de-ceased couple fell to the carpet. Sheryl's parents stared up at them as oblivious to what was happening as they'd been when they were alive.

Gilly Boy grabbed a handful of Sheryl's blonde hair, tightly wrapping his fingers into it before he pulled her head back. He spun her around and forced her to bend over the dining room table.

"You're nothing but a stupid cunt," he said.

"Gilly, I don't —"

He shoved her face hard against the oak table. "Don't talk . . . don't . . . talk . . . don't. . . ."

Gilly Boy used his free hand to unbuckle his belt, unfasten his jeans, and free himself from his shorts. He reached under Sheryl's flower-print housedress and flipped it up on her back. She wore pink cotton panties and he hooked one finger under the waistband and pulled them down off of her buttocks and down her thighs.

Sheryl braced herself against the table. "I won't shut up!" she shouted as she struggled. "I won't let you do this! I won't!"

Gilly Boy found his blade, snapped it open, and held it against the underside of her right breast. "I'll cut it off. I swear to Christ, I'll cut it off!"

He shoved into her from behind, riding her as if she were a bucking bronc, her hair the reins that he used to hold her in check, the knife waiting to impale her if she didn't do as he said.

The sex was hard, and wet, and rough, and she screamed and he roared, and it ended. It had always been hard, and wet, and rough, ever since that first time when they were teenagers and he'd done her in the garage of her parent's house.

She'd fought him then, really fought him, and she still had scars on her right breast and her thighs where he had cut her. She'd told her parents and they'd done nothing, afraid of Gilly Boy and his cousin even then, and ever since then he'd had her any time he'd wanted her.

She didn't know any other way, and she didn't know any other man, and for that reason she would do anything to keep Gilly Boy out of prison, even if it meant lying to the police.

Especially if it meant lying to the police.

Later, alone in his basement, Nikki's killer opened up his switchblade and carefully cleaned it, assuring himself after a half-hour's work that he'd eliminated all traces of the girl's blood. Then he looked over at the one red shoe, re-membering how it had been that night and wondering again why he'd taken it. He didn't need any souvenirs, certainly didn't need anything that would tie him to that night and that room and that girl, and he knew he had to find someone else to take the fall for her death. Someone to take a long, hard fall.

Three people were murdered before noon the next day, finally establishing a new homicide record for the city, one the tabloids would play up in screaming bold headlines. A Korean greengrocer received a single shot from a .22 in his right eye, the bullet ricocheting inside his skull until his brains turned to mush; a young mother received thirty-two stab wounds in her upper torso following a rape while her infant son slept less than six feet away; and two winos fought over a bottle of Thunderbird until one of them sliced the other's throat with the jagged edge of the broken bottle after they dropped it. Sooner or later each of their files would cross Lieutenant Castellano's desk, he would review them, and then he would decide which cases deserved additional attention.

The Lieutenant sat alone in his office, the door shut to mute the sounds of the squad room. He wore his dead sister's silver locket on a necklace tucked under his crisp white shirt. She'd been wearing it the day she disappeared and it had not been recovered at the crime scene. Only he and Ricken-bacher knew how he said he'd recovered it.

They had spent three months tracking a serial killer responsible for the murders of at least two dozen young women, ultimately identifying him as an accountant who had lived all of his life within six blocks of Castellano's parents.

They'd jimmied the lock on the accountant's back door and entered the house without a search warrant, careful to avoid leaving fingerprints as they searched for the killer's stockpile of mementos. Most serial killers keep souvenirs of their crimes in order to relive the events in private, and the two cops found a treasure trove of women's jewelry in the man's bedroom.

Before long they left the house the same way they'd entered and returned to the unmarked car they'd parked at the corner. Castellano showed Rickenbacher the locket he said he'd found while poking his finger through a tangle of necklaces.

"Your sister's?" Rickenbacher asked.

Castellano nodded, closed his fist around the locket, and sat silently. Two hours and a Thermos full of coffee later, the accountant returned home. As he pulled his late-model station wagon into the drive, Castellano started the un-marked car and pulled it into the drive behind him.

Rickenbacher climbed out of the car first. "Excuse me," he said. "You got a moment?"

The accountant glanced from one man to the other, realizing they were police even before Castellano identified himself by flipping open the worn leather wallet containing his badge. The accountant broke for the house, dropping his briefcase and a folder of loose papers on the concrete walk as he ran.

The two cops followed, kicking the folder's contents across the lawn.

The accountant still held his keys and he jammed one in the back door lock, twisting and throwing his weight against the door in one quick movement. Then he was inside, the door slamming shut behind him as he jerked a butcher knife from the knife rack on the counter.

Rickenbacher hit the back door at full speed, his weight splintering the door jamb and driving the door crashing against the wall. The window shattered, sending broken glass across the linoleum. Rickenbacher lost his balance and crashed into the counter on the far side of the kitchen.

Castellano entered immediately behind Rickenbacher, his sidearm drawn and ready. The suspect had turned, knife held confidently in his hand. He found himself between the two cops, unable to decide which one to attack — the big one closest to him or the smaller one with the gun.

Before Castellano could steady his aim, Rickenbacher turned and swung one meaty fist into the side of the account- ant's head. The accountant dropped to the floor, his knees suddenly made of rubber.

Rickenbacher cuffed him, then pulled him off the floor and sat him in one of the kitchen chairs.

When the accountant came to, Castellano placed his service revolver against the man's temple and cocked the hammer.

The accountant sat perfectly still, his wrists shackled behind his back.

"Don't do it," Rickenbacher said. "It isn't worth it."

"It is to me."

The accountant licked his lips. His eyes darted back and forth, unable to focus his gaze on either cop.

Rickenbacher said, "There's a better way."

"How?"

Rickenbacher made his partner step away from the serial killer, then he retrieved the keys to his handcuffs and unfastened them from the accountant's wrists.

"What the fuck are you doing?" the accountant screamed.

Rickenbacher stepped away from him, then pulled his service revolver from its holster and held it by the barrel.

"It's your only chance," Rickenbacher said, then he threw the handgun toward the man in the chair.

Startled, the accountant reached out, catching the gun in mid-air. Castellano squeezed the trigger of his service revolver three times, sending a trio of wad-cutters through the man's chest and spraying his remains across the kitchen.

As Castellano slipped his sidearm back into its holster, Rickenbacher turned to his partner. "Hit me."

"I can't."

"Hit me, you spic fuck!"

Castellano cocked his right fist back and planted it on Rickenbacher's jaw. Rickenbacher stepped backward from the force of the blow.

"That the best you can do, asshole?"

Castellano hit him three more times before Rickenbacher dropped to his knees. The first uniformed officers on the scene found Rickenbacher rubbing his swollen face and the paramedics took him to the hospital to receive attention for a fractured jaw.

Castellano and Rickenbacher had closed out seventeen of the two dozen cases in which the accountant had been a suspect, including the death of Castellano's sister. If anyone had noticed that Maria had been stabbed to death and the other sixteen girls had been strangled, no one mentioned it.

Later, Internal Affairs ruled that Castellano had used justifiable force but they continued to question Rickenbacher about how he'd lost his weapon to the alleged killer.

Rickenbacher stonewalled the officers from I.A. but they monitored his work for the next three months, finally writing him up for excessive use of force during the arrest of a child molester.

That's when Rickenbacher resigned.

Chapter 7

"I've no relatives in the city," Cove said on the other end of the phone line. "I told you that before. No relatives and no friends. Not even an old neighbor who moved north."

"Any former classmates of Katherine's who might have come here after graduation, maybe for college?"

Cove denied the possibility. "I can't think of anybody she knows who might have moved to the city."

"Have you talked to her friends?"

"Some," Cove said. "Mostly I've talked to their parents. Nobody knows why she left."

Even though they'd covered the topic before, Rickenbacher thanked his client. He'd hoped that by returning to the same questions he might get different answers. He hadn't. Cove had repeatedly assured Rickenbacher that Katherine had no ties to the city; no friends, no former classmates, and no ambitions for the theater or any of the other careers that brought doe-eyed young women north to seek fame and fortune.

"If she had no reason to come to the city, what reason did she have for leaving home?"

"Not a one," Cove insisted. "She had everything she wanted. She didn't have any reason to leave."

Circles.

Rickenbacher and his client talked in circles.

Bleach sat across the table from Lieutenant Castellano. Sergeant Kowalski stood behind the mulatto pimp, his beefy arms folded across his chest.

The Lieutenant slid an 8"x10" photo of Jane Doe 43's mutilated body across the table toward the mulatto pimp. "You know her?"

Bleach glanced at the dead girl's photo, a flicker of recognition and anger disappearing quickly. "Never seen her before."

"I've three people who say she worked for you, Warren," Lieutenant Castellano lied. He had spoken to four pimps already that morning and none admitted to ever having seen the dead girl.

"That so? What they names?"

"They say she's been working for you for a couple of months now. What happened, you get tired of her?"

"I didn't have nothing to do with that." Bleach pointed at the photo.

"With what?"

"Killing that girl. I didn't have nothing to do with that."

"When's the last time you saw her?"

"I never seen her."

As the Lieutenant leaned across the table toward Bleach, Sergeant Kowalski placed one beefy hand on the pimp's shoulder.

"You've got one last chance to come clean," Lieutenant

Castellano said. "Otherwise I let the Sergeant finish the discussion."

Bleach looked over his shoulder nervously. Kowalski smiled lopsidedly and tightened his grip on the pimp's shoulder.

When the Lieutenant slid his chair backward and stood, Bleach said, "I didn't know she was dead. I didn't know nothing about that."

"What do you know?" Castellano returned to his seat.

"Coupla night ago, a guy I know come to me, say he want some virgin meat. I show him Nikki. He pay me, I never see her again."

"What's Nikki's last name?"

"Don't have none. She just Nikki, like Madonna just Madonna, like Cher just Cher."

"What did you think happened to her?"

"Hell, I don't know. I think maybe she run home."

"This guy, what was his name?"

Bleach said, "I say too much. I want my lawyer."

"This is just a friendly conversation, Warren. You haven't been charged with anything."

Sergeant Kowalski's grip tightened even more. Bleach winced.

"Get my lawyer."

Castellano stood, straightened the creases in his pants, and walked out of the interrogation room. While waiting for Bleach's lawyer to arrive, he had a few of his desk-bound officers call both the public and private organizations again, asking for information on black-haired teenagers whose names were a variation of Nikki. Before long his desk held a stack of paper — faxes, photocopies, and handwritten notes — all leading to the same lack of a conclusion. None of the Nikkis, Nicoles, Nicolettes, or Nicolinas matched Jane Doe 43.

After talking to Cove, Rickenbacher spent time cleaning his apartment and piling his dirty clothes into a single heap. Then he showered.

With what remained of his hair still damp, Rickenbacher carried two armloads of dirty laundry to the washing machine downstairs, then returned to his apartment to wait until it was time to move the wet laundry into the dryer. He sat at the kitchen table sipping hot coffee, smoking a cigarette, and reviewing all his notes. He thought about the snake that kept swallowing its own tail until it ceased to exist. The Katherine Cove case reminded him of that snake and he worried that at any moment the slender threads he'd hoped to latch onto would disappear completely.

He phoned Castellano to ask about recent arrests of young blondes, but his former partner wasn't available. Then he phoned a florist he'd once busted for possession and had a dozen roses sent to Jesse at the library.

After moving his clothes from the washing machine to the dryer, he returned to his apartment and discovered the phone ringing. Upon answering, he found himself listening to a woman whose testosterone level had shot out of control during the change of life. She identified herself as Sister Mary Margaret of the downtown Catholic Women's Shelter.

"You've been asking a lot of questions at the shelters," she said. "So I called a friend of mine, Sergeant Kowalski, and he said you're a straight shooter. So here's what I've got for you. That girl you're looking for — the plump blonde — she stayed here for two nights. Her and an armload of paperbacks."

Sister Mary Margaret had just given Rickenbacher his second viable lead and he latched onto it. "When?"

"Six weeks ago, give or take. We don't have a guest registry like the Belmont or the Waldorf."

"What happened to her?"

"She came in late one afternoon, offered help in exchange for a cot. She spent the evening reading stories to some of the children we had staying here. Two nights and she was gone. I haven't seen her since. Neither have the other staffers."

"Can I come down and talk to them, maybe show Katherine's photo to some of your residents?"

"Sorry," Sister Mary Margaret said. "We don't allow men inside the building. Too many of these women have been beat up, raped, assaulted."

"But —"

"Look, I wouldn't have called you at all if Sergeant Kowalski hadn't given you the thumbs up. You take what I've given you and be glad you got it."

She hung up abruptly.

"Mr. Canfield?" Lieutenant Castellano asked when his knock was answered by a trim middle-aged man of indeterminate ethnic background.

"Yes?" Canfield said. He wore tight-fitting black jeans, silver-toed black cowboy boots, and an unbuttoned black silk shirt open to expose a paucity of chest hair.

The Lieutenant flipped open a battered brown leather wallet to reveal his gold shield. Canfield had seen badges before and he didn't bother to examine this one.

Canfield's wife called from somewhere inside the house. "Who is it, honey?"

Castellano said, "We'd like to ask you a few questions." He indicated Kowalski standing patiently behind him.

"About what?"

"Your activities a few nights ago."

Canfield's wife called out another question.

He ignored her a second time. "Is there someplace better we can do this?"

"Outside."

Canfield began buttoning his shirt, then yelled over his shoulder. "I'll be outside."

"You understand you're not under arrest —"

"Sure, no problem," Canfield said, interrupting the Lieutenant. "What's your question?"

"We're investigating the death of a young woman."

"And?"

"We think you may have known her."

"I know lots of young women, Lieutenant. Some old ones, too."

When the Lieutenant mentioned the Grafenberg Hotel where Canfield had taken his most recent virgin, Canfield said, "I've been there a few times."

"Three nights ago?"

"I'm not sure," Canfield said. "Did somebody register under my name?"

"Some joker with a sense of humor registered as the Marquis de Sade. Then he cut the girl up pretty good." Castellano straightened the cuffs of his sleeves. "You were seen in the neighborhood."

"Is that all? I'm seen in a lot of neighborhoods, Lieutenant." Canfield smiled. "If that's all, Lieutenant, I've things to do inside."

"That's all," Castellano admitted. "For now. But I'll be back to talk with you later."

Canfield turned and stepped into the house. After Canfield closed the door between them, Castellano smiled. He'd found his viable suspect. Now he could begin assembling the information sufficient for an arrest warrant.

Rickenbacher had trouble starting his van, and when the engine finally caught, he had trouble keeping it going. He'd never been good with machinery, so he called his brother-in-law from the Doughnut World on Broadway and scheduled an appointment to have the younger man give the van a thorough inspection.

Then he continued on toward the county morgue where he'd have the opportunity to view the most recent batch of Jane Does.

J esse had the day off and she took advantage of the warm weather to go jogging. She knew she couldn't compete with all the pretty young girls who jogged just to be seen, and she knew she could never compete with the serious runners. Instead, she dressed comfortably in a tight-fitting blue sports bra that prevented her breasts from jarring painfully as she ran, loose-fitting running shorts that let the breeze glide up her thighs, and well-worn jogging shoes that had cost a week's salary when they were new. She pulled her hair back in a ponytail and held it with one hand until she could slide a rubber band into place around it.

Jesse had a six-mile course, five of the miles through the park. She would run the first two miles, then walk one, run two more miles, then walk the last one home if some idiot van driver didn't try to run her down. It was one of the hazards of city jogging, and one to which she'd never quite grown accustomed.

After locking her apartment door behind her, Jesse taped her apartment key to the inside of her right ankle, smoothed her crew sock over it and then headed down the stairs.

Running usually let her clear her mind, but that day it didn't do her any good. Memories of Rickenbacher kept tumbling over one another as she ran toward the park.

She'd met Rickenbacher and his partner her first night at Doughnut World when she'd nearly spilled hot coffee all over the big man. He'd been quick with a joke and a smile, and he'd left a tip completely out of proportion to his order. She hadn't felt nearly so bad when he returned the following night, ordered coffee again, and she'd managed to pour all of it into the cup.

If she'd noticed the wedding band on his left hand, she'd ignored it, and she'd surprised both of them a few months later when she invited him back to her apartment at the college.

They'd made love that first time in her twin bed. Bob Dylan stared down at them from a wall poster, Janis Joplin screamed at them as a Big Brother and The Holding Company album played on the turn table in her roommate's bedroom, and strawberry incense filled the air. He wasn't the first person she'd ever made love to, but her one encounter with Eddie Futch in the back seat of his father's Lincoln after the Senior Prom didn't seem as significant after she'd felt Rickenbacher's manhood fill her.

It had continued like that for quite some time — her roommate closing her bedroom door when Rickenbacher arrived, his partner covering for him during his visits — until his wife learned of their relationship and gave Rickenbacher an ultimatum. He returned to his first wife, their marriage surviving less than two years after that, but by then Jesse no longer had contact with Rickenbacher and knew no one who did.

As she passed the lamp post at the northwest corner of the park, Jesse slowed her pace and began walking.

"Lieutenant Castellano?" A deep, slow voice asked the question, and when Castellano identified himself, the voice continued. "This here's Bubba Rogers, Sheriff down in Bullfrog Junction, Mississippi, and we ain't had but six missing young'uns in the nineteen years I been on the force and I understand you might have one of 'em up there in your part of the country."

"How's that?" Castellano asked.

"Jimmie Stovall's boy, Selwyn, he's a real whiz kid with these new computers and all, he just finished hooking up one of these pee cees that got windows or something and a modem that can talk to computers all over the country and all and he was telling me how he could look for missing persons so I told him to give a look-see for the Ainsworth girl that disappeared about a year ago and lo and behold I think maybe he found something."

"Ainsworth?"

"Nicolette Ainsworth."

Nikki.

The Lieutenant asked, "Black hair, mid-teens?"

"Yup. Pretty as a picture, she's the Magnolia Blossom Queen two summers back and then about a year ago she up and left town. People said it was an abduction, but you know how people gossip. She always talked about becoming an actress and, hell, we ain't even got a community theater down in these parts."

"What do you have for me? Photos?"

"Yup."

"Medical history?"

"Yup."

"Dental records?"

"Hell, there ain't but one dentist in town," the Sheriff said. "I take it from your questions that I should get the family pastor involved."

"How's that?"

"I'm supposin' our Nikki's no longer among the living."

Castellano described the nature of Nikki's death and the other law enforcement officer sighed heavily. Then the Sheriff said, "This is the part of the job I hate most."

Before he rang off, Sheriff Bubba Rogers promised to have the necessary documentation in Castellano's hands by the next morning.

O ff-duty cops had been hanging out at a hole-in-the-wall bar named Piggy's since before Rickenbacher joined the force. Ephram "Piggy" Goldstein, a corpulent Jew with a ring of nappy hair around the crown of his bald head, had recently begun spending most of his time in a beach-front condo in Florida. He'd left the day-to-day management of the bar to his daughter Ella, a horse-faced blonde with sad eyes and a pair of natural endowments so large most men didn't look at her face. She stood behind the bar pouring drinks.

Rickenbacher found an empty stool next to Sergeant Kowalski and straddled it. When the sergeant looked over at him, Rickenbacher said, "Sister Mary Margaret phoned."

"She's a good woman. I went to school with her kid sister." Kowalski lifted his beer mug and drained the last of it.

"Buy you another?" Rickenbacher offered.

Kowalski shrugged and Rickenbacher motioned for Ella Goldstein's attention. As soon as she looked at him, Rickenbacher pointed to Kowalski's empty mug and held up two fingers.

"You buying something, or you just being friendly?" Kowalski asked after his empty beer had been replaced.

"Just being friendly," Rickenbacher said. "Unless you know something I need to know."

"About your missing girl?" Kowalski pushed his beer mug around on the bar, spinning the handle from the left side to the right. "Just that you're damned lucky Mary Margaret remembered her and thought to ask me about you."

Rickenbacher lifted his beer mug and sipped from it. Beer foam stuck to his upper lip and he wiped it away with the back of his hand.

"Your girl's probably turning tricks by now," Kowalski said. "I wouldn't be surprised to find her cut up in some hotel room one of these days."

"Like the Lieutenant's Jane Doe?"

"He's hung up on this one," Kowalski said. He lifted his beer and drained half of it before continuing. "Says the girl reminds him of his kid sister, the one who died."

"He told me she's tore up so bad you couldn't tell what she looked like."

Kowalski shrugged. "She was." He took another slug of beer. "Some hick sheriff faxed us a picture of the girl."

Rickenbacher finished his beer, dropped a five on the bar for horse-faced Ella, then stood. To Kowalski, he said, "Thanks again for talking to the sister."

"Hey, she didn't know much," Kowalski said.

"Still, it helped."

Rickenbacher left the sergeant sitting at the bar and made his way outside. He had lined up an appointment with a potential client and he only had fifteen minutes to get there.

Carlos introduced the two men and then moved away as Rickenbacher slid into the dimly lit booth. Whatever Canfield had wanted a private dick for, the bartender wanted no part of it.

After he had explained his situation to Rickenbacher, Paul Canfield drummed his fingers on the table top. "I didn't kill her."

"You might plead to statutory rape."

"I didn't know she was underage," he said.

Rickenbacher asked, "Wouldn't you be better served by a lawyer?"

"I've got one, but he won't get his hands dirty."

"And I will?"

Canfield peeled ten fifties from the roll he kept in his pocket and placed them on the bar by Rickenbacher's drink. "That's the retainer. You find the guy who did her and get me off the hook, there's ten times that amount to come."

Rickenbacher looked at the money: five hundred to walk away with, five thousand more if things worked out well. "So what do you do?"

"I buy things and I sell them," Canfield said, not quite answering the question.

"What kind of things?"

"I'd really rather not answer that," Canfield said.

"Ever done time?"

Canfield shook his head. "Look, I'm not going to sit here and try to snow you into thinking I'm some saint. I've done a few things that could send me away, but I've never killed a woman."

"She wasn't a woman," Rickenbacher said. "Just a little girl."

"And I don't plan on going down for murder just because some asshole cop has a hard-on for me."

"That asshole used to be my partner."

"Look," Canfield said, "I don't care if the Lieutenant and you swap blow jobs. I asked around, people said you shoot straight. That's all I want. A square deal because I don't think I'm going to get one with the cops."

The phone rang, the only sound in the bar while Rickenbacher thought. Canfield had lied to him more than once during their conversation, and Rickenbacher knew it. What he didn't know is whether Canfield lied about the girl. Still, it wouldn't hurt him to ask a few questions, hear what the answers were. Rickenbacher knew he didn't really want the case, and took it anyhow. He pocketed the money. "I'll ask a few questions, see if anything turns up."

"Good."

Rickenbacher slid from the booth and looked down at

Canfield. "There is one thing, though."

"What's that?"

"I find out you did it and I'll put you away myself."

Rickenbacher turned and started to walk away. Carlos called out his name, then handed him the phone.

"I have information about a matter close to your heart," said a familiar, but not immediately recognizable, male voice when he answered.

"Yeah?"

"Meet me out back in ten minutes."

A lead pipe crashed against Rickenbacher's neck and he dropped to his knees in the garbage-strewn alley behind the Fuzzy Clam, two doors down from the Muff Inn.

"It's nothing personal," said the vaguely familiar voice he'd heard on the phone. "It's just business."

The pipe caught him one more time and Rickenbacher fell face-first into the wet remains of someone's discarded leftovers. During the next hour, two winos walked past him, one stopping long enough to rifle his pockets and retrieve a wad of fifties from his pants and a pair of crumpled twenties from his wallet. One of the Fuzzy Clam's bartenders nearly tripped over Rickenbacher as he lugged a pair of bulging trash bags to the dumpster behind the strip joint. After discarding the garbage, he stopped, squatted down to take Ricken-bacher's pulse, then went inside to phone the police.

Lieutenant Castellano visited Rickenbacher in the hospital later that night. The big man occupied one of four beds; the other three remained empty.

"You see who hit you?" the Lieutenant asked, certainly not the first police officer to ask him that question since he'd been admitted to the hospital.

Rickenbacher started to shake his head, then decided against it. "No."

"You see anything at all?"

"Nothing. He caught me from behind."

"Why were you in the alley?"

"Meeting someone."

"Who?"

"Guy with a sap."

"Lead pipe," Lieutenant Castellano said. "We already found it."

Rickenbacher shrugged.

"Can you tell me anything about your assailant?"

"He was shorter than me."

"Shit, most people are," Castellano said. The Lieutenant began pacing the room, his hands clasped behind his back as he walked to the window, then back to Rickenbacher's bed. "So why do you think so?"

"Two blows, the first to my shoulder like he couldn't reach my head."

"He say anything?"

"No." Rickenbacher didn't tell the Lieutenant that his assailant's voice seemed familiar.

"Think it was a mugging?"

"Why?"

"The first officer on the scene found your wallet about three feet away. No money, no credit cards."

"I don't have any credit cards." The ones he usually carried didn't have his name on them.

"How much cash did you have?"

"Five hundred and some change," Rickenbacher said.

"Anything else you want to tell me?"

"About what?"

"Your new client, you overgrown fuck! You were seen talking to Paul Canfield about ten minutes before you were cold-cocked in the alley, seen taking money from him." Castellano had stopped pacing. "Canfield's a prime suspect in the Ainsworth girl's murder. I can place him at the Grafenberg Hotel with the girl the night she died."

"Says he didn't do it."

"I say different."

"I only promised him I'd ask a few questions."

"They'd better be the right questions," Castellano said, "'cause this guy's going down."

The Lieutenant stared at his former partner for a full minute before a pudgy blonde nurse interrupted. "He needs to rest now."

"I was just leaving," the Lieutenant told her. To Rickenbacher, he said, "Can I call someone for you?"

Rickenbacher thought about Jesse for a moment, remembering her touch, her taste, her smell. "I've been seeing Jesse again."

Castellano stared at the big man, now trapped in a hospital bed. "She's brought nothing but bad luck."

"Not so bad," Rickenbacher protested.

"Your first wife, then your retirement fund," Castellano said. "That's two strikes. You going for three?"

"My first marriage was on the rocks anyhow. If it hadn't been Jesse, it would have been someone else."

"Your second marriage wasn't so hot, either."

"And I gave up my retirement fund voluntarily."

"So, do you want me to call her, let her know you're in here?"

Rickenbacher thought about it for a moment, then he said, "No. I'll tell her about it later."

"Suit yourself," Castellano said before he turned to leave. "You remember anything else, you let us know."

Rickenbacher had an I.V. drip inserted into one of the veins in the back of his left hand and the nurse injected a painkiller into the saline mixture feeding into him.

While she took his pulse, he asked for a sleeping pill.

"You can't go to sleep, Mr. Rickenbacher," the nurse explained. "We're watching you for signs of a concussion."

Gilly Boy Thomas sat in the front seat of his Chevrolet, idly picking his teeth with the point of his switch-blade. In the park across the street from him, a pair of pathetically-thin women jogged past. They were talking and he could hear their voices through the open window of the car.

"— Mutual Funds, according to my broker."

"I'm just not ready to invest."

"When, if not now?"

"Thirty's still three years away, maybe I'll start worrying about retirement then. Right now I want to live. Condo, nice car, good clothes —"

And then they were past Gilly Boy and he watched their boney butts until they disappeared around a curve. He spent the next forty minutes watching joggers before deciding the park he'd chosen was too busy and too well lit. He brought the Chevy's engine to life, then pulled away.

He had work to do.

The next morning, the coroner confirmed Jane Doe 43's identity as Nicolette Ainsworth of Bullfrog Junction, Mississippi. While Lieutenant Castellano spoke on the phone with Bullfrog Junction's Sheriff, two new patients were wheeled into Rickenbacher's hospital room, one moaning in pain, the other thrashing around in his bed.

Rickenbacher signed himself out of the hospital against the advice of the attending physician. He took a cab to an automatic teller machine to withdraw an even hundred from his checking account and then to his van, still parked a block away from the stretch and featuring a parking ticket under the windshield. On the way home, he stopped to fill a prescription for a week's supply of pain killers and he dry-swallowed two of them.

Mrs. Stegmann saw the bandages on the back of Rick-enbacher's head as soon as he climbed out of his van. Within moments, she bustled out of her apartment, a frayed yellow housecoat wrapped around her, Percival waddling at her heels, and asked, "What happened?"

He told her in as few words as possible, not wanting to repeat everything he'd already told Castellano and not want-ing to involve her in his livelihood. Then he said, "I can't think straight and I feel like I've got a freight train running through my head, worse than any hangover I've ever had."

"Let me help you," Mrs. Stegmann insisted, and even though Rickenbacher had driven himself home, she helped him up the stairs, into his apartment, and into his bed.

Chapter 8

He held Nikki Ainsworth's shoe in one hand and himself in the other, remembering how it had been with her. He kept his eyes closed until he felt himself about to climax, then he shot his wad into the toe.

After he finished, he tucked himself back into his jeans and straightened up. He knew he couldn't keep the shoe forever. He had to get rid of it.

He just didn't yet know how.

Walston woke next to the pug-ugliest woman he'd ever seen — uglier still when he finally managed to fish his eye glasses off the night stand and slip them onto the bridge of his oft-broken nose. He'd picked her up at the Fuzzy Clam the night before after ingesting too many C.C.-and-Sevens, and now he regretted his choice of companionship.

She belched, coughed, then rolled over, waking as he had. She rolled to the side and then out of the bed heading for the bathroom. When she stood, her fat hung like an apron, obscuring her pubic region, and her breasts dangled like tether balls from her chest, her nipples fat little stubs like chewed-up pencil erasers.

Gilly Boy had visited him at the Fuzzy Clam an hour before closing, forty minutes before he'd picked up the heifer now in the bathroom using the toilet bowel as an echo chamber for the music of her bowels, and he'd confirmed delivery of an important package. Bicycle couriers ferried the material around town for them and Walston's three associates waited in hotel rooms for the deliveries. Walston rarely touched any part of the process himself, preferring to let three ex-cons with no hope of a better life take all the risks.

Rickenbacher sat propped up in bed, hot tea and stale cookies from Mrs. Stegmann's kitchen on the night stand beside him, Katherine Cove's file open on the bed between his legs. He read a few of his notes, blinked, then looked away. He couldn't quite focus and his head hurt like hell despite the pain killers he'd been gulping.

Hubert Cove had first phoned Rickenbacher two days after the big man had completed work on a project sub-contracted to him by an agency. It had involved staking out the residence of a woman suspected by her husband of carrying on relations with a neighbor. In the three days Rickenbacher spent drinking cold coffee and urinating into a quart jug, he never once saw the neighbor enter the woman's house. Instead, he'd counted twelve different men arriving, spending no less than one hour and never more than two hours inside with her, and then leaving. Rickenbacher had reported his findings to the agency, collected his check, and then gone back to his apartment to spend time staring at the television.

Cove had offered him a healthy advance, and Rickenbacher had felt no reluctance accepting what seemed to be a simple missing persons case. As soon as the first package from Cove arrived via Federal Express, Rickenbacher knew what Katherine looked like, knew that she'd come to the city with only her babysitting money in hand, and knew that the agency Cove had first hired had accomplished almost nothing.

"Why me?" Rickenbacher had asked during that first telephone conversation.

"You have a reputation."

"For what?"

"Tenaciousness," Cove said. "You don't give up."

"And you think I can do something the agency didn't?"

"I know you can, Rickenbacher, or I wouldn't have phoned."

"Who recommended me?"

"Doesn't matter," Cove told him. "I trust the source."

Rickenbacher knew then that it wasn't anyone at the agency he usually subcontracted work from, and wasn't likely to be any of the cops he'd once worked with. It could only have been a former client.

"I'm a Deacon at the church," Cove told him during a subsequent conversation. "I attend service every Wednesday and Sunday, and meet with the board once a month. Every Friday is Kiwanis, where I'm Treasurer, and every Tuesday is

Rotary, where I'm Past President. I spend Saturdays working with the mentally disabled, and I'm on the Committee to Resurrect Downtown. The new Wal-Mart seems to have sucked downtown dry. Four local businesses have closed their doors since the Wal-Mart opened, and two have moved to neighboring towns."

"What do you do in your spare time?" Rickenbacher asked.

"Golf."

"You're too good to be true," Rickenbacher told his new client.

"How's that?"

"You ever spend time with your daughter?"

"She attended church with me twice a week, and most Saturdays, too."

"Working with the retards?"

The outrage in Cove's voice rang false. "They're not retards," Cove insisted, "they're mentally challenged."

Rickenbacher had known other parents like Cove, parents whose full lives left little room for their children. Still, it didn't seem like much of a reason to leave home. Nothing in the agency's report indicated an abusive environment, nothing indicated a troubled childhood, nothing indicated anything other than an upper middle class existence in a moderate-sized midwestern town.

The agency report was as bland as white bread and about as exciting to read as a parts catalog. Despite the pounding in his head, Rickenbacher thumbed through everything until he found the copy of Katherine's neatly-typed letter to her father, and he read it for the tenth or eleventh time since receiving it.

"Dear Father," it began. "I am not the daughter you expected me to be. I lived life your way for as long as I could, but no more. I must move from under your shadow and I must learn to cast my own." Her signature, including a tiny heart where the dot over the i in Katherine should have been, followed.

Rickenbacher didn't like Cove because he'd lost his daughter and didn't know why. Fathers should know their own children.

Sergeant Kowalski found Canfield sitting in the Muff Inn, nursing a beer and staring at a stripper with hair the color of rust. It cascaded in loose curls down to her lightly-freckled shoulders, and it puffed out in a V-shaped steel wool pad at her crotch. She wore a tiny silver loop through her pierced left nipple. Some women's breasts bounce up and down, some swing from side to side. Hers seemed to do both at once and they fascinated Canfield.

The Sergeant Mirandized Canfield and escorted him out the door before the dancer finished her routine. Soon Canfield sat in an interrogation room staring across the table at the Lieutenant, Sergeant Kowalski behind him. His switchblade had been confiscated and sent to Forensics, and while Canfield sat in the interrogation room, officers with a search warrant were ransacking his home despite the protests of his wife.

"I know you've been read your rights and you understand them, but I'd like to go over everything again," Castellano said. He had a sheet of paper on the table in front of him and he glanced at it. "That okay with you?"

Canfield nodded his assent.

"I need to hear it."

"Sure," Canfield replied. "Go over it again."

Castellano read from the paper, interrupting himself to ask questions. "You have the right to remain silent. That make sense to you?"

"Sure."

"If you give up the right to remain silent, anything you

say can and will be used against you in a court of law. With me so far?"

"Yeah."

"You have the right to speak with an attorney and to have the attorney present during questioning. If you so desire and cannot afford one, an attorney will be appointed for you without charge before the questioning begins. Got that?"

"Got it."

"Do you understand your rights as I have read them to you?"

"Yeah."

Castellano spun the paper around and slid it across the table. He retrieved a slim gold pen from his shirt pocket and placed it on the paper. "Sign at the bottom indicating that you understand your rights. Fair enough?"

Canfield glanced at the page, then signed his name at the bottom and slid everything back to the Lieutenant.

"You're a smart guy, right?"

Canfield shrugged.

"When we spoke the other day, you said you didn't know anything about Nikki Ainsworth's death."

"That her name?" A open pack of filtered cigarettes lay in the center of the wooden table and Canfield reached for them. "You didn't tell me her name last time."

"I've got two witnesses who can place you at the Grafenberg Hotel the night she died, one who says he saw you with Ainsworth."

Canfield correctly surmised that the Lieutenant meant the greasy little hotel manager who'd rented him the room and Bleach, the pimp who'd rented him the girl. "So?"

"You were the last person who saw her alive."

Canfield leaned forward. "Except her killer." Then he leaned back, shook a cigarette free from the pack and lifted it to his lips. Around the filter, he asked, "Got a light?"

Later, after Canfield's statement had been typed and signed, Kowalski carried it into Lieutenant Castellano's office.

"He seems pretty cock-sure of himself," Kowalski said.

Castellano said, "Canfield took her to the room and she didn't come out alive. We've got witnesses to that. Hell, he admitted that he took her there. So he says he didn't kill her? He hasn't got an alibi worth squat, the knife in his boot could have been the murder weapon —"

"Forensics hasn't confirmed that yet," Kowalski interrupted.

"There isn't even reasonable doubt. He did it, he's going down for it."

Despite Mrs. Stegmann's objections, Rickenbacher went to the city jail to meet with Canfield and Canfield's oily-faced lawyer after a late-afternoon phone call roused him from bed.

"My wife is pissed," Canfield told the two other men. "She says the cops tore up the house."

"They find anything?" Rickenbacher asked.

"There wasn't anything to find. I made sure of that."

"Did they say they found anything?"

"I don't even know what they were looking for." Canfield shook his head and the others waited until he continued. "There's one problem."

"What's that?"

"They took my knife. A switchblade."

"And?"

"I stuck her with it."

"You stabbed her?" The lawyer's face went white. There were some things he preferred not knowing about his clients.

"I didn't stab her," Canfield protested. "I stuck her under the chin to get her attention."

"This your idea of fun-and-games?" Rickenbacher asked. "You told me you didn't do the girl. Why are you jerking us around now?"

"Look, a drop of blood, and that's all. I didn't stab her."

"And you didn't clean the knife."

"I tried, wiped it on a towel before I left the room. Still, how good a job could I have done?"

When Rickenbacher returned home there were two messages on his answering machine. The first, from Elmer Hapgood, simply said, "That girl you was looking for came in today."

Jesse had left the second message, but only her name and number. Rickenbacher looked at his watch and realized the time to return Hapgood's call had long passed and contact would have to be made in the morning. He picked up the phone and dialed Jesse's number.

She answered sleepily and when she recognized Rickenbacher's voice, she said, "You didn't return my call right away. I thought your machine broke."

"I was working."

"Find her yet?"

"No luck at all."

"Not as easy as finding me, was it?"

Rickenbacher mumbled his assent.

"Now what?"

"How's that?"

"Us."

Rickenbacher didn't know what to say. He hadn't thought of himself and Jesse as "us" in years.

"You haven't said anything."

"I know."

"You brought back a lot of memories, seeing you like that, going for hot dogs and all. You sent roses. What happens now? Do we see each other again, or what?"

"Let's take it slow," Rickenbacher finally said.

"Slow," Jesse repeated. The phone line popped and crackled with static for a moment while she sat silently on the other end of the line. "I won't wait for you. Not again."

They said good-night to one another and Rickenbacher tucked himself into bed, wrapping his arms around one of the pillows and remembering what it had been like with her.

Rickenbacher's first stop the next morning was Happy's Books.

"Who're you supposed to be, the Mummy?" Hapgood asked when Rickenbacher pushed his way inside, his head still heavily bandaged.

Rickenbacher shook his head negatively, then stopped when it felt like a jackhammer had started up inside his skull.

"That girl you're looking for was in yesterday," Hapgood said. "She bought a couple of romance novels."

"And?"

"She was wearing those Spandex pants and had a bicycle helmet on."

"You see which way she went?"

"No, but she dropped this." Hapgood reached under the counter and when his hand came back into view, his fingers were wrapped around a bookplate. He handed it to Rickenbacher and apologized for the foot print obscuring the top left corner. "She was wearing one of those hip sacks," Hapgood continued, "and after she paid for the books she reached in it for some of these. Pasted one inside the front cover of each book. This one must have dropped to the floor but I didn't see it until about an hour later when I came around the counter to help a customer."

Rickenbacher examined the bookplate. On each corner frolicked a cat and in the middle someone had typed an address — an address not far from the bookstore.

Rickenbacher thanked the old man with a crisp twenty before leaving.

Barely half the mailboxes in the apartment building's lobby had names on them, and none had Katherine Cove's. Rickenbacher climbed stairs and counted unnumbered doors until he arrived in front of apartment 5G.

The big man used an expired MasterCard with someone else's named embossed on it to jimmy the lock on the apartment's heavy wooden door. Once inside the tiny efficiency, he flipped on the overhead light. He found a neatly made single bed, an overstuffed chair, a flexible brass clamshell floor lamp, a four-drawer dresser with a stack of bricks in place of one leg, and a bookcase built of peach crates and filled with second-hand paperbacks, their covers stripped by unscrupulous booksellers who returned the covers for credit while selling the stripped books at a discount to unsuspecting readers. Mostly romances, the books were organized by author, then by title, and inside the front cover or on the first page of the stripped books was a bookplate matching the one Hapgood had given him.

The kitchen, hidden from the rest of the room by a moth-eaten blue curtain, contained a chipped porcelain sink, a four-burner electric stove, and a half-size refrigerator. The cabinets above the sink contained mis-matched place settings for two, including plates, salad bowls, and coffee mugs, three cans of tomato soup, a family-sized box of generic brand corn flakes, and a Tupperware tub of sugar. The refrigerator contained an unopened quart of 2% milk and three peaches.

On the kitchen table sat the manual typewriter that had

been used to type Katherine's name and address on the bookplates. Next to it lay a TenSpeed Deliveries business card.

In the cabinet under the bathroom sink, Rickenbacher found an opened box of Tampax, two rolls of toilet paper, and a pan half full of dirty water from the leaking drain. The medicine cabinet above the sink had been stuffed full of expensive cosmetics and most of them threatened to topple out when he opened the cabinet door. A toothbrush and a tube of toothpaste, carefully rolled up from the bottom as it had been used, stood upright in a pale blue ceramic mug on the corner of the sink. In a white wicker basket next to the toilet lay months-old copies of *The Advocate*, *Cosmopolitan*, *On Our Backs*, *Out*, *Sassy*, and *Seventeen*, dog-eared from frequent readings. A pair of beige pantyhose hung over the shower curtain rod.

Rickenbacher returned to the main living area and lifted the blind on the apartment's only window. He found himself staring at a brick wall less than six feet away. He lowered the shade, took one last look around, then let himself out of the apartment.

Downstairs, Rickenbacher located the building's superintendent and asked, "Who's in apartment 5G?"

"It's vacant, man."

Rickenbacher stepped forward, causing the super to step backward. "Don't screw with me."

"You a cop? Let's see some I.D., raghead."

Rickenbacher stepped forward again. The super stepped backward and his shoulders struck the wall.

"Half the apartments in here are vacant, man," the super said. "I ain't lyin'."

"I just want to know who's in 5G."

"Look, man, I don't know. I don't ask her name and she don't tell me."

"What's she look like?"

"Stone fox, man."

"Young? Blonde?"

"That's right, man. You know her?"

"And you don't know her name?"

"That's the best way, man," the super said. As Rickenbacher turned to leave, the super asked, "If you ain't a cop, where you from?"

The big man never answered.

After dropping his van off at his brother-in-law's garage, but before hailing a cab, Rickenbacher cut away as much of the surgical dressing covering his wound as he could, then he covered the rest with a baseball cap turned backward so the bill shielded his neck.

Thick steel plates covered the street and the cab bounced over them on its way across town. When the driver finally pulled to the curb in front of the 501 building, the meter read eight-and-a-quarter. Before climbing out of the taxi, Rickenbacher gave the driver a ten and told him to keep the change.

Inside, a fat man chewing the stub end of a cheap cigar thumbed Rickenbacher toward the rear after he asked to speak to one of the couriers. A sinewy blonde sat in an overstuffed chair watching the Howard Hawkes version of *The Thing*, her back to the door.

"Katherine?"

Kat stiffened but did not turn.

"Katherine Cove?"

Rickenbacher placed one hand on her shoulder. She stood suddenly and spun away, out of his grasp.

"Who the hell are you and what do you want?"

Two other bicycle couriers remained in the office with Kat. One watched warily from his position on the couch. The other stood, placing himself between Rickenbacher and

Kat. Though he didn't stand as tall as Rickenbacher, his arms and shoulders were thick from repeated visits to the gym. "You heard the lady."

Rickenbacher identified himself and his occupation over the other man's shoulder. "Your father hired me."

Kat bolted toward the back door. Rickenbacher tried to follow and found his path blocked by the thick-chested courier.

"Leave the lady alone."

"This ain't your concern," Rickenbacher said.

The thick-chested hero made a fist and drew back his arm. Before he could fire the punch he'd so carefully prepared, Rickenbacher placed one meaty fist in the courier's gut, doubling him over. Rickenbacher stepped past him, around the other courier who still sat on the couch, and followed Katherine out the back door, too late to stop her.

He saw the rear wheel of her bicycle as it disappeared around the corner. He ran toward the mouth of the alley, then stopped. Without his van, Rickenbacher had no hope of catching the girl.

He walked down the alley until it spit him out on the street where he hailed a taxi. He didn't have to chase Katherine Cove; he knew where she lived.

Rickenbacher considered phoning Jesse, but decided he didn't want her involved in the case any further than she'd already become involved. He'd asked for her help once and didn't intend to do it again.

Instead, he phoned Colette, confirmed that she was home, then met her at her apartment and briefly described the situation.

"I scared her," Rickenbacher finally concluded, "and she ran."

"So what can I do?" Colette asked.

"I need to talk to her about her father. I need you to make her understand I'm not the enemy."

"Why me?"

"I trust you. Maybe she will, too."

Colette examined Rickenbacher carefully. "You scare a lot of people."

"I never scared you."

Colette smiled. "I never met a man big enough to scare me."

They used Colette's car, an import too small for Rickenbacher to fit comfortably inside without opening the sun roof so the top of his head could stick out. They stopped first at TenSpeed Deliveries and Colette confirmed with the cigar-smoking fat man that Katherine had not returned to work, then they drove to her apartment and found it unoccupied.

"It's a big city," Colette said. "She could be anywhere."

They cruised the neighborhood, looking for bicycles, and stopping each time they found a ten speed chained to a light pole or a hydrant or a bench. They finally located Katherine in a diner, where she sat at the counter picking at a B.L.T. and sipping diet cola through a straw.

Colette went in alone and slipped onto the empty stool beside the young girl. Katherine glanced up at her.

"There's other places to sit."

"I want to sit here, next to you."

"You a dyke?"

"I just want to talk for a minute."

The waitress came over. Colette ordered coffee, black.

"About what?"

"Your family."

"Haven't got a family," Katherine said. "Just a father."

"He's worried about you, wants you to come home."

"How do you know that?"

"A friend of mine told me."

"So, who's your friend?"

Colette signaled Rickenbacher through the glass. He saw from outside and moved toward the door.

"He'll be here in a minute, Katherine."

"You know my name. What's yours?"

Colette introduced herself. "My friend tried to talk to you earlier. You ran away."

Rickenbacher stepped into the diner just then and Katherine saw him. "Jesus, not him."

Katherine started to push herself off the stool. Colette put one hand on the girl's arm to stop her.

"It's okay. He won't hurt you."

Rickenbacher eased onto the stool on the other side of Colette, away from Katherine. The waitress saw him and brought two cups, filling them both with a tepid brown liquid resembling coffee.

"There's nobody between you and the door," Colette said. "You can leave any time and we won't stop you."

Katherine glanced towards the entrance, then looked back at Colette. Rickenbacher silently sipped his coffee and listened to the two women.

"If this is some weird come-on for a threesome —"

"It isn't," Colette interrupted. She introduced Rickenbacher and the three of them talked for nearly an hour before Colette suggested they continue their conversation in private. The big man paid for Katherine's dinner and their coffee before they left the diner. Colette lived closest, so they loaded Katherine's bicycle into the trunk of Colette's import and went there.

Colette had decorated her two-bedroom apartment tastefully. She no longer entertained clients, so she no longer needed the trappings of the profession. Instead, the place looked like the lodgings of a female middle-manager, the furniture expensive but tasteful, mostly oak in the living room. The only thing seemingly out of place was a cordless phone with a headset so she could take calls that were transferred to her from the 900 number in a building eleven blocks away.

After only a few minutes in the apartment, Katherine said, "I'm not going back and you can't make me."

Rickenbacher picked up the phone and dialed a number that had grown more familiar over the preceding few weeks. When Hubert Cove answered, Rickenbacher said, "I found her."

"Thank God."

"If you insist," Rickenbacher said, "but I did most of the work."

Cove ignored Rickenbacher's wisecrack. "Where was she?"

"Here," Rickenbacher said. "In the city."

"Is Katherine okay?"

"She's fine."

"Then send her back."

"I can't."

"I want my little girl home."

"She doesn't want to return."

"She doesn't have a choice." Cove's voice raised an octave. "She's my daughter."

"She's an adult now. She can make her own decisions."

"Where is she now?"

"She's with me," Rickenbacher said as he glanced over at Katherine.

"Let me talk to her."

Rickenbacher covered the mouthpiece of the phone. "He wants to talk to you."

Kat shook her head.

Rickenbacher uncovered the mouthpiece and said, "She doesn't want to talk to you."

"Put her on the phone, damn it. What am I paying you for?"

"To find her," Rickenbacher explained. "I found her. My job's done."

"You sanctimonious ignoramus —"

Rickenbacher dropped the phone into its cradle. To Kat, he said, "Your father's not happy."

"He wouldn't be happy if he won the state lottery."

"Tell us about it."

"Another time, maybe," Kat said. "You got anything to drink? I'm thirsty."

"Orange juice, diet cola, water," Colette said.

"Diet. You got ice?" When Colette confirmed that she did, Kat said, "In a glass with ice, then."

Colette returned a moment later, the cold soda in her hand.

"You were a hard woman to locate," Rickenbacher told her.

"I like it that way. I didn't think my father would try so hard to find me."

"Why's that?"

Kat ignored the question. "I get twenty percent off my rent as long as I pay cash every month, don't put in a phone, and don't receive mail," Katherine explained. "Nobody knows I'm there, landlord don't have to report my rent as income. It's a good deal for both of us."

Kat flopped onto Colette's couch and picked up a two-day-old newspaper from the coffee table. The paper had been left folded open to the story about Jane Doe 43's murder. After she read it, Kat said, "I was there."

"Where?" Rickenbacher asked.

"The hotel where that happened." She tossed the paper toward him and shuddered. "I made a delivery on the same floor where that girl died."

"What time?"

"I don't know." She shrugged. "Late."

"You see anybody?"

"The guy I delivered to." Kat gnawed at the ball of her thumb as she thought. "And a guy coming out of 4B."

The man she described couldn't have been Canfield.

Carlos stood behind the bar at the Muff Inn and eyed the greasy-haired blond with the crudely-etched tattoo on the back of his left hand. When the shot glass in the blond's hand finally emptied, he offered a refill.

"Look, you Mexican fuck, when I want another I'll blow beans out my ass so's you'll hear the toot and know to come runnin'."

Carlos' eyelids narrowed. "I'm not Mexican."

"Like I care what kind of illegal spic you are?" Gilly Boy Thomas laughed. "You ain't nothin' but lower'n shit, takin' away all the nigger jobs."

Six years tracking insurgents through the Guatemalan jungle while waiting for an opportunity to slip north had not prepared Carlos for life in America. In the Guatemalan jungle, he was feared, but in America he served drunks and worried about immigration officials sending him home.

"You're still starin' at me, spic boy," said Gilly Boy. "You want I should cut your *cajones* off, make a fuzzy coin purse for your woman?"

Another customer signaled for Carlos, waving an empty beer bottle. Carlos stepped back from the greasy-haired blond and turned away. At home, he never would have backed down from a challenge, but at home men were real men, not like in America.

Kat lay in bed staring up at the ceiling. She'd talked to Rickenbacher and Colette for much of the evening, finally returning home after midnight. They'd dropped her and her ten speed off at the curb and waited until she'd entered the building before driving away.

Her father had paid the big man to find her and he'd found her. She could run, but she could not hide. Anywhere she went, her father would send someone looking for her. She wondered if Rickenbacher would give her father her address. She wondered if she would come home from work one evening and find her father standing at her door. She wondered if she could ever leave her past behind.

"I don't think he did it," Rickenbacher told the Lieutenant as they glanced over the menus at Good Eats. "I've got a witness says she saw someone else come out of the room about an hour after Canfield said he'd left it."

"Who?"

"The girl I was looking for."

Carlos sat at the counter with his back to them, listening and remembering the photo of Katherine Cove he still had tucked under the cash register at the Muff Inn.

"What was she doing in the hotel that night?"

"She's been working for TenSpeed Deliveries as a bicycle courier. She made a delivery."

The waitress squeaked over and took their order. After she turned and squeaked away, Castellano asked, "Has she ever met Canfield or seen his picture?"

"Nope."

"So I can put him in a line-up and you're sure she won't finger him?"

"I'll take my chances."

Carlos finished his burger, dropped a crumpled five on the counter to cover the bill, and headed for the door.

"I've got him in lock-up right now," Castellano said. "You bring your girl down to the station and let's see what happens."

"Give me an hour."

Rickenbacher left Good Eats without ordering, took a cab to Katherine's apartment, and woke her up by pounding on the door.

"Now what do you want?" Kat asked when she saw the big man standing in the hallway outside her apartment.

Rickenbacher explained and before long Katherine stood in the tiny room, surrounded by Rickenbacher, Kowalski, Canfield's attorney, and a night school graduate from the District Attorney's Office. She stared through the one-way glass at the five men lined up in the other room facing her. Although she recognized none of them, she stared at Canfield, three cops in plain clothes, and a wino who earned extra money sweeping out the station and filling in on line-ups. She shook her head.

"Look again," Sergeant Kowalski said. The Lieutenant had been called away moments before Katherine and Rickenbacher's arrival and he had yet to return. "You're sure the man you saw coming out of 4B that night isn't in that line-up?"

"I've never seen any of those men before."

"Cut him loose," Canfield's lawyer said.

"We've got two other witnesses," Kowalski said. "The pimp and the hotel manager."

"It ain't enough."

Rickenbacher took Katherine's elbow and eased her from the room while the sergeant and Canfield's lawyer sprayed testosterone at one another. In the hall outside, she asked, "Did I say the right thing?"

"Only if you told the truth."

The other door opened and the suspects from the line-up began filtering out.

"Damn," Rickenbacher swore. He spun Katherine around so her back was to the five men and the uniformed officer escorting them, but he wasn't fast enough. Canfield

saw him and called his name. Under his breath, Rickenbacher whispered, "Stay here. Don't turn around."

"That her?" Canfield asked. The uniform had cuffed
him for the trip back to the holding cell and when he pointed
toward Katherine, he had to lift both hands. "That my angel
of mercy?"

Rickenbacher stepped into Canfield's line of sight. "You
didn't see anything."

"I'd like to talk to my lawyer," Canfield told the uniform
who had stepped behind him and placed a hand on his
shoulder. "I'd like to talk to the little bastard before he leaves
me here."

"I'll tell him," the uniform said.

Nicolette Ainsworth's casket remained closed, de-
nying her loved ones the opportunity to convince themselves
that she had, indeed, passed from this life. She'd flown home
that morning, arriving at Memphis International Airport just
as dawn crept over the horizon and gave birth to the day.
Pickergill's had a hearse waiting at the airport for her and
she'd ridden to the funeral home with Clavius, a middle-
aged black man who had a taste for unfiltered Camel's and
the ironic. He played Harry Chapin's "Taxi" over and over
again on the hearse's cassette player, singing along and laughing at the thought of ever flying again after totaling his
father's crop-duster and mangling his own left leg.

He delivered her to the funeral home, then stood aside
with his cap in hand as her family arrived to mourn her
passing. Nicolette's mother wailed, clawing at the casket as
if to open it until Nicolette's father took his wife's shoulders
firmly in his callused hands and drew her away. Her older
brother — the one who had been quarterback on the high
school's only championship team and who now had two
children of his own and worked as a mechanic for the Dodge

dealer — stood silently in the corner, holding hands with each of his children. His wife, a former cheerleader who had ballooned with each pregnancy and who now resembled nothing less than the Pillsbury Doughboy on a bad hair day, whispered repeatedly in his ear. "I told her not to go. I did. I told her nothing good would happen if she left. I told her."

Nicolette's younger brother sat alone on one of the metal folding chairs in the back until the sheriff — third cousin to the girl's mother — noticed the boy and sat on the empty seat beside him. The boy looked up, his pale blue eye filled with unshed tears. "Why'd they kill my sister, Sheriff Bubba? Why'd they do that?"

Answering was the part of the job he hated most, and he held the boy close, letting tears no longer youthful stain his uniform.

Nicolette left home to become an actress. She returned to play the staring role in a family drama none too common in Bullfrog Junction. The last murder known to local residents had occurred more than two years previous, when a Yankee and a local boy had disagreed over the right-of-way at a four-way stop. Despite the NRA sticker on the good old boy's bumper and the gun rack inside his pickup, he hadn't been prepared for the Yankee with the handgun who'd decided it was his day to enforce traffic laws.

Nicolette's story would be told and retold throughout town and would grow with each telling, embellished by each teller, until she became the star she had dreamed of becoming.

Memories of Nicolette's death haunted her killer and he woke bathed in sweat, damp sheets tangled around his legs. He had not meant to kill the girl, only to frighten her with the knife, as he had frightened the others.

Canfield had slipped out of the hotel room without

locking the door and he had slipped inside, finding the girl curled on the bed in a fetal position, crying soft southern tears. The room smelled of sex, the odor as raw and carnal as any animal's and it excited him. He removed his overcoat, hanging it from the door knob. Then he slipped out of his clothes. As he approached the bed, she did not acknowledge him, did not even stir.

Black hair, long as a winter's night, hid her face and he brushed it away, revealing tear-stained cheeks and a bloody stain under her chin.

He brandished the knife, threatening her, but she seemed not to notice his presence. He grabbed one wrist and pulled the girl's hand away from her face, trying to force her onto her back, but she resisted. She didn't fight, not like some of the others had fought. Instead, she stared at him, unseeing.

Her face.

He forced her onto her back, forced her arms to her sides, straightened her legs on the bed, parting them slightly. Her young breasts flattened against her chest, her areolas twin pink oblongs against her pale skin. The dark mat of her pubic hair lay damp and tangled at the juncture of her thighs.

Her face, so much like the first.

Still she'd said nothing, done nothing to acknowledge his presence, so he'd used the razor-sharp edge of the blade to gain her attention, drawing a thin line of blood for three inches along her jaw line below her left ear.

She'd screamed then, surprising him.

And he knew why the face spooked him.

He plunged the blade into her.

Wanting her to stop.

Then plunged the blade into her again.

Wanting her to go away.

And again.

Wanting her to disappear.

Not stopping until his arm tired and he realized that she hadn't moved and he wore her blood like a body suit.

He did not stop to think, then. He dressed, pulling his clothes on quickly, covering himself. When he stumbled on her shoe as he hurried to the door, he picked it up and shoved it into his overcoat pocket along with his switchblade.

Then he was gone, out the door, down the hall and down the stairs, until he emerged into the night. He hurried away from the hotel, unaware that he'd been seen.

Until later, when he'd learned about Katherine Cove.

During the night, a six-year-old girl choked to death when her nine-year-old brother found their parents' sex toys and strapped a ball gag onto her while she slept, a pair of skinheads beat a homosexual to death with baseball bats while a crowd of people watched without intervening, and a discharged postal employee carried an M-16 into the substation where he'd worked and killed his former supervisor and two former co-workers before turning the gun on himself. Then the sun rose.

The last dancer of the night, a woman with skin the color of weak tea and a heart as black as coal, finished her set at the Muff Inn and sashayed from the stage. Ben Kirkland brought the house lights up, nearly blinding two medical supplies sales reps who sat in a corner arguing about the new discounts offered by one of the premier manufacturers of autoclaves. They finished their beers, rose from the table, and stumbled out to meet the day. An Italian kid with stringy black hair and bad complexion began clearing away the residue of a long night. In the other strip joints along the stretch, variations of the same events took place.

Chapter 9

Two days later, Kat found Rickenbacher sitting at the end of the bar at the Muff Inn. He had his hand wrapped around a cold bottle of Budweiser and he raised it to his lips for a long draw as she crossed the room toward him. On the stage, a slim black woman with skin as smooth and black as an eggplant, contorted her body in strange and erotic ways.

Kat slipped onto the empty bar stool beside Rickenbacher and he glanced down at her. An unfamiliar bartender appeared and she ordered orange juice.

"Been looking for you all morning," Kat told the big man after the bartender slipped away. "I tried calling, but I just got your machine."

"You ready to go home now?"

Kat snorted. "In your dreams."

"So why come looking for me?"

"I think someone's been following me."

"Why?"

"How the hell should I know why?" Kat snapped.

Rickenbacher shook his head. The music stopped and the black stripper hurried off stage. An anemic young woman with straw-blonde hair and coal-black pubic hair replaced her. "What makes you think someone is following you?"

"I just feel it."

"How?"

"Like when you think someone is watching you and you

turn around and there's someone there." Kat sipped at her orange juice.

"So who've you seen?"

"A skinny guy. Taller than me, shorter than you," she said. "I've never seen his face, but I'm sure it's been the same guy each time. He's followed me home, knows where I live."

"Why are you telling me?" Rickenbacher finished his beer, slid the empty bottle across the counter, then pointed at it. The bartender quickly replaced it with a freshly-opened bottle.

"I thought maybe I could get you to do something about it, get rid of the guy or tell him to bug off or something."

"Do you know my rates?"

Kat shook her head so Rickenbacher told them to her. She said, "I can't afford that."

Rickenbacher shrugged, then lifted his new beer to his lips. The dancer on stage smiled at him and shook her breasts in his direction, her stubby nipples aimed at him like twin gun barrels.

"Well, shit," Kat said, her voice rising an octave. She pushed herself off the stool and put her fists on her hips. "If you won't help me, who will?"

Rickenbacher turned to face her. "Go home to your father."

"I *can't!*"

"Why the hell not?"

Kat glared at the big man, then she spun on her heel and stormed out of the Muff Inn.

The bartender yelled after her. "Hey! Hey! What about the juice!"

Rickenbacher turned to face him. "Put it on my tab."

During the previous few days Rickenbacher had dealt with two highly disappointed clients. Cove's daughter had been located but she would not return home, and Canfield sat in a jail cell unable to post bail. His own financial well-being had suffered as well. Cove had refused to advance any additional funds, and he had lost Canfield's retainer after he'd been bashed in the head behind the Fuzzy Clam. He nursed his second beer for another half hour before finally heading for the door.

ieutenant Castellano slapped the folder down on his desk. "Damn it, Kowalski, can't we do any better than this?"

Since arresting Paul Canfield and charging him with the First Degree Murder of Nicolette Ainsworth, their investigation had stalled. Upon the advice of his attorney and with no admission of pandering, Bleach acknowledged seeing Canfield and the dead girl together only a few hours prior to her death. The hotel manager picked Canfield out of a line-up and identified him as the man who'd registered as Marquis de Sade. Canfield's switchblade had been confiscated and a spot of blood found on the point had been identified as Nicolette's. Yet, they had not located the dead girl's missing shoe. Katherine Cove claimed to have seen a different man leaving the hotel room where Nicolette died at least an hour after Canfield claimed to have left. The forensic pathologist assigned to the case claimed that Canfield's switchblade could not have caused most of the wounds on her body, and she was doubtful it could have caused the rest.

Kowalski shrugged. "It's enough to take to court."

"But it may not be enough to convict," Castellano said. "I want the son-of-a-bitch off the street forever."

"We've done the best we can."

"Do better."

"We have more than a dozen on-going investigations," Kowalski reminded the Lieutenant. "We're stretched mighty thin."

Castellano ran his fingers through his hair. "I know. I know."

Kowalski glanced at the folder on Castellano's desk. "I'll see what I can do." He stopped after he opened the door, turning to face the Lieutenant. "It sure would help if we could find her other shoe."

Castellano's eyes narrowed to slits and he nodded slowly.

Nikki's killer had burned everything — his jacket, shirt, tie, slacks, even his underwear and his hundred-dollar loafers.

Everything except her shoe.

He'd hidden it in his basement.

Rickenbacher had taken her to dinner the previous evening, and Jesse still felt an internal glow. Their date had ended with a passionate kiss at her apartment door, but she had not invited the big man inside. As much as she wanted him and as much as she knew he wanted her, she also knew their relationship had to develop slowly. Twice before everything had crashed down around them and she did not want their relationship to fall apart a third time.

Rickenbacher walked a different road than most men, a road that led to a destination only he understood. It was what attracted her to him and what repelled her as well. She let a tiny sigh escape and she shook her head.

She closed the file on her computer screen and gathered up two children's books. The children were looking forward to story hour and she looked forward to reading.

After Sergeant Kowalski vacated his office, Lieutenant Castellano reopened the case file for Nicolette Ainsworth and began rereading. He'd gone over most of the information a dozen times, but he hadn't paid sufficient attention to Katherine Cove's statement. Kowalski had taken it a few minutes after she'd examined the men in the line-up and had been unable to identify Paul Canfield.

Katherine's statement was short. A bicycle courier for TenSpeed Deliveries named Raul Rameriz had picked up three packages, each with a different destination. Two of the packages had been dropped off at the TenSpeed office and the dispatcher had given her the one destined for the Grafenberg Hotel, Room 4D. Another officer had confirmed the details of Katherine's statement through discussion with the TenSpeed dispatcher and through examination of the dispatch records for that evening.

She rode her bicycle to the Grafenberg, chained it to the hydrant out front, then went inside to find room 4D. Another officer had spoken to the hotel manager, who confirmed Katherine's arrival but not her departure.

Katherine had taken the elevator upstairs to the fourth floor and had delivered the package to Mr. Smith. She described Mr. Smith as a greasy-haired blond male with an upside-down cross tattooed on the back of his left hand. The Grafenberg's manager confirmed that the room had been rented to a man who identified himself as John Smith, but he claimed the man who rented the room was a fat, balding Jew.

As Katherine stood in the elevator waiting for the doors to close, a man exited room 4B, pulled the door shut very quietly, then turned away from her and began walking quickly toward the stairs.

She described the man as slender, with greying black hair and tanned or darkened skin, wearing an overcoat or trench coat. That was the only time she had seen the man, and then she'd only seen his face in profile for a moment. Her description was sufficiently vague that it described at least a hundred men, but Castellano suspected she could identify the killer if she ever saw him again.

Castellano closed the folder and stared at the photo of his sister. She'd been so beautiful.

Rickenbacher's van remained in his brother-in-law's shop so he had to take a cab to the city jail. The cab's driver seemed to bounce through every pothole between Rickenbacher's apartment and his destination and when he finally pulled to the curb in front of the jail, Rickenbacher didn't bother tipping the driver. He received an upraised middle finger but by then he had his back turned and had made it halfway up the steps.

Inside, he asked to see Canfield and was escorted into a room containing a dozen wooden tables with foot-tall wooden barriers bisecting each of them. Anything passed between visitor and prisoner had to be passed over the top of the barrier. A uniformed officer sat at one end of the room picking at his nails, a haggard man and a pock-faced woman argued quietly over the top of one table while at the only other occupied table a lawyer repeatedly tried to explain the basic precepts of law to a client too dense to understand his situation. Rickenbacher found a seat at the table farthest away from everyone else, and he waited patiently until Canfield arrived.

"Well?" Canfield asked as he dropped into the hard-backed wooden seat across the table from Rickenbacher.

"I've asked around. No one saw you after you claim to have left the hotel."

"I told you. The manager had his back turned when I went out. He was watching television in his room behind the desk."

"What was he watching?"

"How the hell should I know? I didn't stop to ask."

"Then where'd you go?"

Canfield's story never changed. The girl was still alive when he left her. He took the elevator down to the lobby and walked out the door to the street. He didn't remember seeing anyone as he walked the block to his parked car, climbed in, and drove away. He drove for an indeterminate amount of time, then went home. His wife had already fallen asleep and she didn't stir when he showered, toweled himself dry, and climbed into bed beside her.

Over the past few days, Rickenbacher had retraced Canfield's steps a dozen times, questioning every wino, hooker, and street person in the neighborhood around the hotel. Those who were coherent remembered nothing special about the night of Nicolette's death, nor did they recall seeing Canfield. They did recall two beat cops, a plainclothes detective, and the trash collectors whose banging around woke them before dawn the next morning.

"You're going down for this one," Rickenbacher said.

"I don't have to," Canfield said. "That girl of yours is my alibi."

"Is that why you're having her tailed?"

Canfield's eyes narrowed. "What are you talking about?"

"She says someone's been following her."

"That doesn't have a damn thing to do with me," Canfield said. "In fact, if there is someone following her, maybe you better see to it that she's taken care of. Anything happens to her, I could wind up somebody's girlfriend."

"A tough guy like you?"

Canfield snorted. "You ain't seen tough until you've seen what comes in here."

"I take care of her, you going to pay the freight?"

"Whatever it takes. Just be sure she testifies."

Rickenbacher had what he'd come for. He left Canfield sitting at the table, made his way outside, and took a cab to his brother-in-law's garage.

Castellano stopped at home on his way to visit Gilly Boy. He spent less than ten minutes collecting a few household items he thought he would need later, and he stashed them in the trunk of the unmarked car the department had assigned him. Then he drove to Gilly Boy's home and found the younger man sitting on the top step of his front porch, picking his fingernails with the point of a switchblade. They both knew possession of the switchblade violated the terms of Gilly Boy's parole, but Gilly Boy made no move to conceal the blade.

"I know you were at the Grafenberg," Castellano said as he climbed the seven steps to the porch. He brushed a spot clean with the palm of his hand and then sat down beside Gilly Boy. "I've got a witness."

"The delivery girl," Gilly Boy said without looking up.

"She puts you in the right place at the right time."

"Little bitch." Gilly Boy finished with his fingernails, closed the switchblade, and slid it into the right front pocket of his tight-fitting jeans.

"What were you doing there that night?"

"Working."

"Doing what?"

Gilly Boy shrugged. "Things."

When Castellano waited for Gilly Boy to elaborate, Gilly Boy asked, "Haven't you already collared the guy that did it?"

"Maybe it took two guys," the Lieutenant suggested. "You doubled-up with your cousin once, why not again?"

Gilly Boy glared at the Lieutenant. "You gonna read me

my rights?"

"You're not under arrest."

"Then why you asking me these questions?"

"I just want to know who you saw there that night."

"You want me to say I saw this other guy?"

Castellano didn't answer.

"Show me his picture. Tell me his name. I got nothing to lose, do I?" Gilly Boy asked. "I roll on him or you'll find a way to take me down, too."

"Gilly Boy, there's only one person who saw you there that night." The Lieutenant stood, brushed dirt and chipped paint from the seat of his slacks, and then straightened the creases.

Rickenbacher glared at the bill his brother-in-law handed him and said, "I didn't pay this much when I bought it from you."

His brother-in-law shrugged. "You should take better care of it, then."

Rickenbacher pulled out his wallet, paid his brother-in-law in cash, then climbed in the van and drove away muttering nasty things about auto mechanics.

Gilly Boy watched the Lieutenant's back as he returned to the tan sedan he'd arrived in, and he watched as the Lieutenant started the car's engine and then pulled away from the curb. After the unmarked car disappeared around the corner, Sheryl came out of her house next door and crossed the two yards.

She stood at the bottom of the steps and looked up at Gilly Boy. "What did he want?"

"There's a witness, says I was at the Grafenberg the

night that girl bought it."

"You were with me that night," Sheryl insisted. She had repeated the story so often that she almost believed it herself.

"Your word against hers."

"What are you going to do about it?"

Gilly Boy shrugged. "I've got two choices. I roll over on this other guy or I get rid of the broad who says she saw me there that night."

"Gilly." Sheryl reached out to stroke his cheek with the back of her hand. "Don't mess it up, Gilly. I don't think I can live if they send you back."

Gilly Boy slapped her hand away.

Nikki's killer spent half-an-hour arranging everything just so. Then he closed the door and walked away as quietly as he had arrived.

Rickenbacher found Katherine Cove at TenSpeed Deliveries, received a withering glare from the courier who'd tried to protect her the last time he'd visited, and he took her aside to talk.

"If someone's really watching you, maybe you'd better not go back to your apartment."

"Why the change of heart?"

"Someone else agreed to pay the bill."

"My father?"

Rickenbacher shook his head. He said, "I'll pick up anything you need."

"Where will I stay?"

"My place."

"Forget you, bud."

The fat guy behind the counter made him use the pay phone, and Rickenbacher placed two calls. During the second, Colette agreed to let Katherine stay with her for a few days.

"This makes us square, don't it?" Colette asked.

"Close enough," Rickenbacher said.

"Then bring her by. I'll get the spare room ready."

"What about my stuff?" Kat asked on the drive to Colette's apartment.

"I'll pick it up later," Rickenbacher told her. "What do you need?"

Kat listed a number of items, from fresh clothes to a half-dozen paperback novels.

Rickenbacher used Katherine's keys to unlock her apartment door. Then he reached inside and flipped on the overhead light. As soon as he did, the room exploded in a fireball. The thick wooden door protected Rickenbacher from the force of the explosion, but his sleeve caught fire. He slammed the door shut and quickly stripped off his trench coat, dropping it to the floor and stomping at the flames.

At the end of the hall, a fire alarm had been mounted and he hurried toward it, grabbing the handle and jerking it down. Nothing happened. Smoke billowed out from under Katherine's apartment door. Rickenbacher pulled the alarm a second time.

He turned and pounded on the first apartment door he saw, then he crossed the hall and pounded on another. He yelled, cursed, and screamed as he made his way down the long hall until doors began to open. By then thick smoke hung in the air and Rickenbacher coughed as he inhaled it. He quit pounding on doors and ran toward the stairs, not stopping until he pushed his way out of the building four floors below and saw a fire engine rounding the corner two blocks away, its siren splitting the still night, its flashing lights reflecting off the buildings on both sides of the street. By then, the entire neighborhood had woken and Rickenbacher slipped away as quickly as possible.

He told Katherine about the fire as soon as he returned to Colette's apartment.

"You didn't save anything?"

Rickenbacher shook his head. "There wasn't time."

"My clothes? My books?"

"All gone."

Katherine collapsed onto Colette's couch, burying her face in her hands. She fought back tears and when she'd won the battle, she looked up at the big man. "I told you someone was after me."

"Somebody wants her dead," Rickenbacher explained to Lieutenant Castellano. "Her apartment didn't detonate itself."

"People know she saw the killer."

Rickenbacher lifted a cigarette to his lips and inhaled deeply, drawing smoke into his lungs. He held it a moment, then exhaled. "I need your help on this one."

The Lieutenant shook his head. Not one strand of hair moved out of place. "Not as long as my prime suspect is your client."

"He didn't do it."

Castellano stood, indicating that their meeting had ended. "You figure it out. Nicolette Ainsworth is dead. She was alive when your client took her into a hotel room and I've got two witnesses who'll say so. All you've got is a scared little girl who says she saw a different man coming out of that room sometime after Canfield claims he left. You ain't got shit and you know it."

Rickenbacher left the Lieutenant's office and made his way to the Muff Inn, where he wrapped his big hand around a cold bottle of Budweiser and sucked it nearly dry.

"It's time to leave," said a familiar voice. It came from across the room. Ben Kirkland stood over a slender drunk. "You've had enough."

After Ben escorted the drunk out the front door, Rickenbacher followed the tattooed bouncer into the back.

"Why'd you do it, Ben?" Rickenbacher had finally remembered why the voice had been familiar and he confronted the squat fireplug of a man backstage at the Muff Inn.

"Like I told ya, it was just business." Ben Kirkland, his arms folded across his wide chest, stared up at Rickenbacher. "For another two hundred, I'd do it again, too. I've got child support payments eating me alive. I pick up extra dough as best I can."

"I was packing five."

"I wish I'd known. It might have been enough insurance to prevent your accident."

The music stopped and the malnourished blonde Rickenbacher had seen on stage a few nights earlier rushed offstage, squeezing between the two men in the narrow hall between the stage entrance and the dressing rooms.

"So who hired you?"

Ben shrugged. "Man called while you were out front with Canfield, said there'd be two hundred in it if I caught you out back and worked you over."

The next stripper stood waiting for her music to begin. As she waited, she rubbed ice cubes against her nipples to stiffen them. When the pounding strains of a Van Halen tune pumped through the Muff Inn's stereo system, she hurried onstage.

"You think I wouldn't figure out it was you?" Rickenbacher asked.

"I counted on you figuring it out," the fireplug said. "Wouldn'ta thought much of you if you hadn't figured it out."

"So why'd this guy want me worked over?"

"Didn't say, didn't ask."

"Just business."

"Yeah. I got no beef with you, Big Dick. Didn't have one before, don't have one now."

Rickenbacher stared down at the man, stared at the Sistine Chapel intricacies of his tattoos and then into the deep pools of the man's eyes. "Next time you think twice about the jobs you do for people."

Ben nodded.

The two men had never been friends, but they had also never been enemies. Like professional boxers, they respected one another and would do what they had to do to win each round if they were matched up in the ring. They knew better than to take their jobs personally.

Rickenbacher turned to leave, but Ben stopped him with a meaty hand on his arm. "You didn't hear this from me."

"Yeah?"

"The guy said he was friends with Mr. Johnson."

"Johnson was scum," Walston explained when Rickenbacher cornered him twenty minutes later. "There's nobody sorry to see him gone."

"Somebody must be," Rickenbacher said. "He had me whacked."

"A disgruntled customer, maybe," Walston explained. "He certainly had enough of them."

"What about you?" Rickenbacher asked. "You do business with Johnson?"

"Not often, and not by choice," Walston said. "I ain't got no beef against little kids."

Rickenbacher met Jesse at a Greek restaurant down the block from her apartment. He arrived ten minutes late, but he carried a solitary red rose he'd purchased from a skinny black kid on the corner.

"I was about to leave," Jesse said as Rickenbacher approached the table.

"Sorry," he said, apologizing for his tardiness. He handed her the rose, then took off his fedora and placed it on the chair beside him. "Business took longer than expected."

"Business before pleasure, then?"

"Not always," Rickenbacher said. "And not now."

"Will I ever be the most important thing in your life?" Jesse asked.

Rickenbacher received a reprieve before he could form an answer. Their waiter stopped at the table, introduced himself as all obnoxious waiters do, and then proceeded to list the evening's specialties.

They each ordered without glancing at the menu, and then suffered through having their water glasses filled, their bread basket delivered, their wine opened, then sampled and served. Finally they were alone again.

"We've been through this twice before," Jesse said. "The third time's the charm, right?"

Rickenbacher smiled. He hadn't had to answer her other question. "The third time's the charm."

"It has to be, right?"

Rickenbacher nodded.

Then their appetizer arrived.

Chapter 10

Dinner had gone remarkably well and Jesse invited Rickenbacher up to her apartment afterward. Once inside, they both realized she wouldn't be preparing coffee.

As the door closed behind them, they came together in an embrace that shed years from their lives, taking them back to when they'd first met and the passion they'd then shared.

Jesse ran her fingers through Rickenbacher's hair, knocking his cap to the floor and sliding her fingertips over the slick spot on the back of his head. She'd not yet seen the top of his head but she knew full well what she felt. The years that had added threads of grey to her hair had begun to rob Rickenbacher of his.

It didn't matter. In the same way that Rickenbacher didn't notice her additional weight, she didn't notice his thinning hair. Instead, she concentrated on the gentleness of the thick, slightly chapped lips that caressed hers and grew moist as their kiss lengthened into a fiery oral dance of tongues.

In the years they'd been apart, they had each been with others, yet none of those experiences intruded as they concentrated on one another. Their fingers found and unfastened buttons, belts, and clasps and she felt his thick hands exploring territory that he knew well.

Rickenbacher lifted Jesse and carried her into the bedroom where he placed her on the comforter, then lay beside her. His hands continued exploring her breasts, her buttocks, her inner thighs. Jesse's pubic mound felt softer, fuller than he'd remembered. Some of the weight she'd gained over the years had settled there, padding her pelvis.

She was soft and moist and ready and Rickenbacher poised himself between her legs. As he prepared to enter her, Jesse stopped him with a light touch. "Do you have any protection?"

Rickenbacher drew back and rolled away from Jesse.

"Don't worry," she whispered. "I do."

Afterward, they lay entwined on Jesse's bed and Rickenbacher stared up at the ceiling.

"Where does this leave us?" Jesse asked. She lay on her side, her head on his chest, her left leg thrown over his.

Rickenbacher didn't respond. Instead, he sat up and reached for his cigarettes. Jesse placed one hand on his arm, stopping him.

"Not yet," she said as she took him in her hand. "We're not finished."

When Rickenbacher finally left, Jesse lay in bed and stared at the wall for nearly an hour. She had never expected him to re-enter her life, and she'd had even less hope of ever sharing a bed with him again. The thoughts that tumbled through her mind confused her in a way that they never had before. Rickenbacher was something from her past, something in her present, but could she reasonably expect him to be a part of her future?

Jesse finally kicked away the covers and climbed out of bed. She pulled on her sweats, taped her apartment key to her ankle, and headed down the steps.

Gilly Boy felt the cool night breeze tickle his hair. It had been a long, hard day, and he'd had too many things to think about. Too many conflicting thoughts had crowded together in his mind and he needed release.

He needed the thrill of the hunt, the thrill of capture. He needed to taste fear, his tongue capturing the sweat of fear, his fingers feeling the trembling flesh of fear.

He needed a woman.

He did not need Sheryl. She was no longer afraid. To her it had become a game.

He waited, leaning against a tree behind a row of bushes. The park was quiet this time of night, but sooner or later a jogger would come past.

Running cleared her head, swept out the cobwebs in her mind, and allowed her to concentrate. Before long, Jesse entered the park from the south, following the same north-bound trail she always followed.

She ran, her running shoes slapping against the pavement in a methodic cadence, her breathing slow and steady. She didn't realize someone had been watching her until he scrambled from the bushes ahead of her, too quickly for her to stop and turn away. He already had the switchblade open and the razor-sharp edge gleamed in the pale moonlight. He caught her arm and used her forward momentum to drive her to her knees, then down on all fours.

The asphalt tore at her kneecaps and the palms of her hands. She bled.

Jesse tried to scuttle away, but he grabbed her hair and pulled her back.

She turned and aimed a fist at his midsection. Missed.

He pulled her to her knees, then held the blade of his knife under her chin as he fumbled with his zipper.

She felt the sharp edge of the blade against her throat, the asphalt hard against her bleeding knees, the stinging pain in the palms of her hands. She knew what was coming.

He finally freed himself. "Eat this."

The blade moved away as he shoved his erection in her face. She protested, turned her head to the side, and when she did he slapped her, snapping her head around the other direction. As her head snapped from one side to the other, she caught a glimpse of a crudely-etched tattoo on the back of her assailant's left hand.

"I told you to eat this."

He shoved himself into her mouth, and she gagged. He slapped her again, and she bit, clamping her jaws shut and grinding her teeth into the soft flesh of his rapidly deflating erection.

He screamed.

And didn't stop screaming until she finally released her oral grip on him and he staggered away, holding both hands to his crotch.

Jesse stumbled to her feet and ran, the blood from his wounds still salty on her lips. She spat and spat again until she had locked herself in her apartment and had gargled away the remains of her encounter with Gilly Boy.

Then she showered, scrubbing away all traces of her assailant. She stayed under the pulsing stream of the shower until the hot water ran cold and goosebumps began to rise.

She brushed her teeth a dozen times, then gargled again.

Later, Jesse sat at a battered desk, a pile of mug books surrounding her and a pinched-faced detective with sour breath standing behind her. He idly clicked a breath mint against his teeth as she stared at one photo after another.

"I didn't get a good look at his face."

"What did you see?"

"His penis."

"How will we identify him?"

"He'll be the only suspect with a mutilated pecker," Lieutenant Castellano said, interrupting them. He'd been passing by the room when her voice caught his attention. He'd turned to look at the woman with Detective Sotherland, then realized why her voice rang the familiarity bell. He'd spent more than one night sitting in an unmarked police car while his former partner played hide the sausage in Jesse's apartment.

"I saw his left hand. He had a tattoo on the back, I think."

Sotherland said, "This isn't your case, Lieutenant. Go back to homicide."

"Jesse's an old friend, Detective. I'll stick my nose in if I choose."

Castellano stared at the older man until Sotherland looked away. "Anything you can do to help, Lieutenant?"

Castellano returned his attention to Jesse. "What about the tattoo?"

"It could have been a grease smudge," she said. "I'm not sure." She described it as a lower-case t, the stem pointing up his arm.

Castellano turned to Sotherland and asked, "Have you phoned the D.A.'s office yet?"

"No, sir, not yet."

"Why don't you get us all some coffee, Detective," Castellano suggested, "and take your time coming back."

After Sotherland left, pulling the door closed behind him, Castellano perched on the edge of the desk and looked down at Jesse.

"You been to the hospital yet?"

"The detective said it'd be a waste of time."

"Why?"

"I showered as soon as I got home, brushed my teeth, gargled."

"What about your clothes?" When she looked him a question, Castellano explained. "The clothes you were wearing when it happened. Where are they?"

"At home, in the bathroom. I just took them off and left them there."

"Good," he said. "Sotherland can collect them later. So tell me what happened."

Jesse repeated the story again, including, at Castellano's prompting, everything she could remember about her assailant. He asked her a few more questions, then he dug through the pile of mug books, selected one and flipped through the pages, finally laying it open in front of her.

"Look through these very carefully," he instructed. He didn't coax her, but soon she'd picked out Gilly Boy Thomas.

"I didn't think I'd seen his face, but I'd swear this is the man."

Castellano nodded. He closed the mug book and set it aside. After a moment of silence during which he straightened his shirt cuffs, he asked, "You intend to prosecute?"

"Absolutely."

Castellano straightened the pleats of his black slacks, then looked at her again. "What kind of a witness will you make, a hooker accusing a guy of rape?"

"Ex."

"Ex what?"

"Hooker. I haven't turned a trick in years."

"What are you doing these days?"

"Librarian," Jesse answered. "Children's section at the Main branch."

Castellano smiled, then asked, "The defense lawyer will try to introduce your past. Maybe he'll succeed, maybe the judge will overrule him. Either way, it'll be in the jury's minds. It'll get back to the library. Then what?"

Jesse sat silent for a moment, reliving the incident in the park.

Castellano interrupted her memory and said, "There may be another way."

"How?"

"Big Dick," Castellano suggested. "You've been seeing him again, haven't you?"

The next morning Castellano visited Gilly Boy's home and asked a few questions. "There was a woman assaulted in the park last night. She says it was you."

"I was here last night," Gilly Boy insisted.

"All night?"

Gilly Boy shrugged. "Spent an hour or so next door."

"Anybody with you?"

"Sheryl."

"What'd the two of you do?"

Gilly Boy smiled. "I'da videotaped everything if I'd known you were coming."

"You couldn't leave well enough alone, could you?" the Lieutenant asked.

"How's that?"

"You fucked with Big Dick's girl."

Gilly Boy's eyes widened slightly.

"He finds out it was you, he'll come calling."

"It wasn't me and he couldn't prove it if it was."

"If I make you pull down your pants, are we going to find out different?"

"You can't make me do that."

Castellano pulled his service revolver from his shoulder holster. He placed the barrel behind Gilly Boy's left ear and cocked the hammer back. Then he whispered carefully, "If I want you to play frog, you'll jump."

Except for the sweat trickling down his forehead and stinging his eyes, Gilly Boy sat motionless until the Lieutenant finally returned his revolver to its holster.

"You need to go home," Rickenbacher explained. He sat on the couch in Colette's apartment, leaning forward with his elbows on his knees. Katherine sat across from him in an overstuffed chair.

Kat said, "I can't."

"You keep saying that." Rickenbacher pushed his hat back, off of his forehead so it perched precariously on the crown of his head. "Why the hell can't you go home?"

"I think I'm gay!" Kat spat at the big man.

"You *think* you're gay? Don't you know?"

Kat didn't answered the question. Instead, she said, "My father's a deacon in the church. How would it look if everyone found out his daughter's a lesbian?"

"Won't he love you no matter what?" Rickenbacher stood up and began to pace across the green shag carpet. He retrieved a half-empty pack of cigarettes from his shirt pocket and shook one loose.

"You should hear him talk about homosexuals. Queers. Faggots. He says they'll burn in hell."

Rickenbacher stopped and turned toward the young woman. "Ironic, isn't it?"

"What?"

"You," the big man said around the filter of the cigarette he'd pinned between his lips. He slipped the crumpled pack back in his pocket.

"Yeah," Kat said. "Ironic. He never thought his daughter would be a lezzie."

Colette had been in the kitchen and she stepped into the living room. When she saw the cigarette dangling from the corner of Rickenbacher's mouth, she said, "Don't light that in here."

Rickenbacher stared at the semi-retired prostitute for a moment, then said, "Ah, shit, not you, too."

"Gave it up when I moved in here two years ago. I'm not about to let you stink up the place."

Rickenbacher sucked on the unlit cigarette and re-turned his attention to Katherine. "Have you ever told your father how you feel?"

"I tried once —"

"Only once?"

"— and he wouldn't listen. He started quoting scripture at me."

"Doesn't the Bible say to love thy neighbor?" Colette asked. She sat on the couch, as near to Katherine as she could get.

"Not if the neighbor's a fag."

"Your father's a real hardliner, then," Rickenbacher said.

"Absolutely."

"Have you ever really given him a chance?"

"Why?" Kat asked. She looked from Colette to Rickenbacher, then back at Colette. "He isn't likely to give me a chance."

"Parents have an infinite capacity for love," Colette explained. "Most of them."

"Yours?"

"Even mine," Colette explained. "I ran away from home when I was sixteen, thinking my parents were the meanest, cruelest people on the face of the earth. Then I met some men who taught me different."

On his way out, Rickenbacher discovered Lieutenant Castellano sitting in a tan sedan with a whip antenna and government plates. He pulled open the passenger door and slid in beside his former partner.

"Nice night," Castellano said.

"Could be better."

"How's that?"

"You could tell me why you're sitting out here."

"You said there was someone following your girl, could mess up your client's alibi. I want to see who it is."

"How'd you know where to find her?"

"Followed you," Castellano lifted the Thermos from between his legs. "Coffee?"

Rickenbacher remembered all the nights they'd sat together drinking coffee and urinating into empty milk bottles so they wouldn't have to leave the car during a stakeout. He said he wouldn't mind a cup and Castellano filled the Thermos' cap with black coffee thick as oil and handed it to Rickenbacher.

"Report's in already on her apartment." The Lieutenant didn't look at Rickenbacher. "Arson, of course. Incendiary device where the light bulb should have been in the ceiling lamp."

"Somebody knew his shit."

"And they found a trench coat in the hallway outside, they think it belongs to the arsonist."

"How's that?"

"The inspector thinks maybe the thing blew up prematurely. Some of the officers on the scene got a description of the guy. Big guy, about your size. There were some credit cards in the pocket of the coat, though, with the name Wilson Tuckman on them."

"They find anything else?"

Castellano shook his head. "Nothing to speak of."

They sat silently sipping coffee until Castellano asked, "She alone in there?"

"Katherine's got company."

"Who?"

"Colette Rees."

"She's still around?"

"Semi-retired," Rickenbacher said. "Does phone stuff these days."

"Tough old bird."

"Bit a guy's dick in half once when he tried to rape her. He's doing seven to ten now. The other inmates call him Stumpy."

"Or girl-friend."

They both laughed.

"So, you seen anybody hanging around?"

Castellano said he hadn't.

"Plan to be here all night?"

"Another hour or so."

Rickenbacher finished the coffee, rolled down the car window and shook the dregs from the bottom of the cup out the window.

"You see anything, you'll let me know."

"Of course," Castellano said.

Rickenbacher opened the car door and slid out.

Before he could close the door, Castellano asked, "You talked to Jesse lately?"

Rickenbacher bent over and stuck his head back inside. "No, why?"

"Maybe you should."

Inside Colette's apartment the two women continued the conversation Rickenbacher had started.

"What makes you think you're gay?" Colette asked.

"It isn't any *one* thing," Kat explained. "It's a lot of things."

"So tell me about them."

"Why should I talk to you?"

"Why not?" Colette asked. "I've seen just about every-thing a man can do to a woman, and I don't blame you a bit if you want to avoid all that. They use you, abuse you, and lose you."

"It's not that."

"Then what is it?"

Kat took her time, but she finally told Colette about the summer between her junior and senior years of high school, when she'd spent nearly three months as a camp counselor at a retreat sponsored by her church.

"I shared a cabin with Monica Baldwin, and it seemed like we had everything in common. She liked what I liked and I liked what she liked and we spent hours talking about everything. One night, about two weeks after I arrived, we were sitting on my bunk in the dark, talking about sex. By then I'd been dating off-and-on for almost two years, and I had kissed maybe a dozen boys, been felt up by three or four of them, but I was still a virgin. Absolutely, completely, no-doubt-about-it virgin."

Kat stopped talking long enough to glance at Colette. The older woman waited for Kat to continue.

"Well, after a while, she asked if I'd ever kissed another woman and I told her sure. I'd kissed my aunts and my grandmother, like that, and she said no, have you ever really kissed a woman and before I realized it her lips were on mine and we were kissing. I was scared at first, but I didn't push her away. I liked it. A lot. And I kissed her back, big, wet, sloppy kisses and before I realized it were laying on my bunk together, our nightgowns pushed off onto the floor. I lost my virginity to Monica."

When she stopped a second time, Colette prompted her gently. "Many women have at least one same-sex encounter when they're young. I know I did."

Kat shook her head. "It wasn't just that one time. It was almost every night after that. For two more months. I couldn't look at boys the same when I went back to school in the fall. I started watching the other girls in the locker room after gym class, wondering if there were any others like me."

"What happened to Monica?"

"She went back home. I never saw her or heard from her again."

"And your father?"

"Never knew. I wasn't going to tell him anything about

it, but I knew I couldn't stay there any longer than I had to. I knew I had to get away."

"What about now?" Colette asked. "You still attracted to other women?"

Kat nodded.

Chapter 11

A message waited on his machine when he returned home, and Rickenbacher returned Jesse's phone call before he even had time to remove his hat. He went to Jesse's apartment and she told him about the attempted rape. He tried to comfort her, but she was beyond comforting. He tried to hold her in his arms, but she pushed him away.

"I've done it for love, and I've done it for money," Jesse said, "but I've never, ever done it because some man forced me to."

She told Rickenbacher what Castellano had said about going to trial, but her voice held no emotion. She even told him the name of the man she'd identified from his mug shot. "I just wish that bastard was dead."

Rickenbacher spent the night sitting on Jesse's couch, listening to her until she finally fell asleep curled up against his chest. He napped off and on throughout the night, snapping awake every time Jesse stirred. He loved the feel of her, the scent of her hair, the way she fit neatly into his arms when he held her. He knew what he had to do, but not how to do it.

The following morning, aware that there was little he could do for Jesse that she would understand, he gave her the name and phone number of a rape counselor he'd once worked with. As much as he wanted to stay with Jesse and spend the day comforting her, there was another woman in his life who needed his help.

Rickenbacher drove home, changed clothes, picked up the .22 and the switchblade he'd obtained a few days earlier, then drove to Lieutenant Castellano's house on a secluded side street. The small front yard had the greenest grass in the neighborhood, all of it trimmed to a uniform one-inch height, and the edging along the sidewalk appeared ruler-straight. A trio of waist-high shrubs on either side of the front steps had been trimmed square, and neither a leaf nor a branch poked out to mar the appearance. Paint peeled from the houses on either side of the Lieutenant's, but his had been freshly painted.

Rickenbacher bounded up the steps, across the porch, and pounded on the door until the Lieutenant groggily answered.

"It's early, Dick," Castellano said through the screen. His pajamas had been pressed and starched and showed little sign of having been slept in.

"You know what happened to Jesse, don't you?"

Castellano ushered his former partner into the living room and took a seat on the couch under a family portrait taken when his sister had finished grade school. "I saw her just after it happened."

"Why didn't you call me?"

"I thought it was her place to tell you."

"Gilly Boy did it, didn't he?"

"There's no doubt in my mind."

"And what are you doing about it?"

"It wasn't a homicide. What do you expect me to do?" Castellano shook his head. "It's Sotherland's case."

"Jesus," Rickenbacher swore. He pushed his hat back and ran his fingers through his thinning hair. "Sotherland can't wipe his own ass without help."

"Besides, the case can't go to court without destroying Jesse's reputation. She'll lose her job at the library. You wouldn't want that to happen, would you?"

Rickenbacher shook his head. Then he paced Castellano's living room, his rubber heels thudding against the highly polished hardwood floor. He'd been in Castellano's living room many times before and little had changed. Though the furniture had been replaced since his last visit, it remained a room that did not invite company. Sparsely furnished with only a couch, a chair, an end table caddy-corner between them, and a console television set on the far side of the room. A reading lamp hung over the chair. The walls, however, could almost be considered cluttered by comparison. Photos of Castellano's family, professionally matted and framed in silver, were neatly arranged on each wall. Only two other things had been framed and hung on the wall: next to the door leading down to the basement were Castellano's discharge papers from the Marine Corps and his graduation certificate from the Police Academy.

"There's another thing," the Lieutenant said. He straightened the *TV Guide* on the end table, squaring the spine with the edge of the table. "Gilly Boy was at the Grafenberg Hotel the night Nicolette Ainsworth died."

"I thought he'd been cleared. His alibi held."

"Your girl saw him there."

"Katherine?" Rickenbacher stopped and turned toward

his former partner, his eyes narrowed to slits. "How do you know?"

"I reread Kowalski's report and matched him up to her description of Mr. Smith, the man she'd delivered the package to."

"And?"

"It's been confirmed already. He was there."

Rickenbacher swore. When he'd started looking for the thread that tied everything together, he hadn't expected to find Gilly Boy.

"What can we do?"

"Me?" Castellano said. He stared up at Rickenbacher. "Not a damned thing. But you —"

Castellano let the words hang in the air, his sentence unfinished, hoping his former partner would understand.

Rickenbacher stopped at Good Eats for Adam and Eve on a raft — scrambled eggs on toast. He'd finished his meal and had started on his second cup of coffee when Ben Kirkland sauntered into the diner and straddled the stool next to him.

"You're up early," Rickenbacher said.

Ben shrugged. The tattoos on his forearms danced.

The waitress squeaked over with a cup of coffee, took Ben's order for steak, eggs, and biscuits, then squeaked away.

"There's been talk," Ben said.

"Yeah?"

"It seems most of Mr. Johnson's friends have disappeared." Ben sipped coffee. "The cops have Johnson's computer files and they're more concerned about covering their asses than in doing anything about you."

Rickenbacher looked down at the squat fireplug of a man beside him. "They'll be back doing the same thing when this all blows over."

"You wipe up the dirt one smudge at a time," Ben said. "First Mr. Johnson, then somebody else, right?"

"Johnson tripped."

Ben smiled. "Maybe the next guy will, too."

Rickenbacher paid his bill, leaving a couple of extra bucks for the waitress with the silver beehive.

H e drove to the TenSpeed Deliveries office and talked to the day-shift dispatcher, an anemic, bespeckled man with thinning black hair and bad complexion.

He asked about the package Katherine had delivered the night Nicolette Ainsworth had died.

"Do you have a search warrant?"

Rickenbacher slid an Alexander Hamilton across the desk.

"If he's got a friend, maybe I could look it up for you."

Rickenbacher slid another ten dollar bill across the desk. TenSpeed's dispatcher folded both bills and slid them into his shirt pocket. Then he turned to the registry and thumbed back to the night of Nicolette's death.

"She made four deliveries that night."

"Mr. Smith at the Grafenberg," Rickenbacher said, narrowing the focus of their discussion.

The dispatcher adjusted his glasses and trailed his finger across the page. "What do you need to know?"

"Where'd the package come from?"

"Three packages, actually." He read the address where the packages had originated and Rickenbacher wrote it on a scrap of paper he'd pulled from his pocket.

"One went to the Grafenberg," Rickenbacher said. "Where did the other two get delivered?"

The dispatcher read off one address, then turned back to Rickenbacher. "The third package was never delivered."

"Why not?"

"Damned if I know." The dispatcher looked down at the registry again, "But the kid assigned that job is working days this week."

He leaned over the counter and called into the courier's lounge. The hero who'd tried to stand between Rickenbacher and Katherine Cove a few days earlier ambled up to the desk. He gave Rickenbacher a nasty glare. When the dispatcher asked him about the undelivered package, the courier said, "There were cops all over the place. I didn't want anything to do with that scene."

He returned to the courier's lounge when the dispatcher dismissed him.

"Where was it supposed to go?" Rickenbacher asked.

The dispatcher gave Rickenbacher an address that he recognized as belonging to Mr. Johnson's office. "We tried to return it to the sender, but couldn't."

"Where's that?"

The dispatcher read off another address, which Rickenbacher noted on his scrap of paper.

"So where's the package now?"

"If the owner hasn't called for it yet, it'll be in the back room."

"Would you look?"

"Alex got any more friends?"

Rickenbacher retrieved his wallet, pulled out a pair of ten dollar bills, and held them up. "Two more, if it's there."

The phone rang. The dispatcher answered it, made a note, then called one of the bicycle couriers to the front desk and gave him instructions. As soon as they were alone again, he walked to a door behind the desk. He opened it, switched on the light, and began rifling through two shelving units full of packages. Over his shoulder, he told Rickenbacher, "You wouldn't believe the crap we have back here, the stuff people ask us to deliver but nobody will accept."

He returned to the desk with a 9"x12" manila envelope,

half an inch thick and sealed with strapping tape. It had been addressed with a black felt-tip pen.

"How often have you lost packages?"

"Not often. Why?"

"You've lost this one." Rickenbacher took the package from the bespeckled dispatcher's hand and dropped the two ten dollar bills on the desk before the anemic guy could protest.

Rickenbacher didn't open the envelope until he'd returned to his van. After examining everything quickly, he drove to the sender's address.

The unlit neon sign mounted to the wall above the boarded-up front window read *Gloria's House of Style*. Rickenbacher received no response when he knocked and when he twisted the front knob he found it locked. He walked around to the alley, counting doors until he felt sure he stood by the rear entrance of Gloria's. Again, he received no response when he knocked.

Rickenbacher glanced both ways, assuring himself that he had the alley to himself. Then he opened the switchblade and used it to pry open the door's lock, snapping off the blade's tip in the process. Once inside, he squinted against the darkness until he found the light switch. Nothing happened when he flicked it up and down.

Without light, the big man picked his way carefully through the storage room through which he'd entered. Once in the main room light filtered in through the boarded-up front window and he could see well enough that he didn't have to squint.

Gloria's had once been a beauty salon with three stations along each wall and a row of hair dryers along the back. Each station included a sink and a small cabinet to contain all the tools of a beautician's trade. The cabinets were mostly empty now, and only one chair remained in place.

An area in the back of the room, next to one of the sinks,

had been thoroughly cleaned, floor swept, and sink scrubbed. Despite the condition of the rest of the room, only the faintest trace of dust covered any surface, as if the area had been cleaned within the past week.

Rickenbacher bent to examine a 3"x5" scrap of paper he found under the sink, the Kodak label clearly evident on the up side of the paper. He used his finger to flip the paper over but saw no photographic image. Instead, he only saw the grey/black of an accidentally-exposed piece of photographic paper. He carefully picked it up and slid it into his pocket.

After another twenty minutes of careful examination, Rickenbacher discovered nothing else abnormal about the room, so he exited the same way he'd entered.

He made two quick stops on his way back to Colette's apartment, one at an automatic teller.

"I stopped at Happy's. He said you'd like these," Rickenbacher said to Katherine as he dropped a trio of romance novels on Colette's coffee table. Then he opened his wallet, pulled out a fifty and a pair of twenties, and handed them to her. "You'll need some clothes, too."

When Katherine didn't take the money from his outstretched hand, Rickenbacher followed her gaze and saw that she was staring at his wallet.

"Who's that beside you?" Katherine asked. She pointed to a picture of Rickenbacher and Castellano back when they'd worn uniforms.

"My former partner."

"He looks familiar."

"Sure," Rickenbacher said. "You saw him at the police station, during the line-up."

"He wasn't there."

"In the room with us," Rickenbacher said, then remembered Kowalski making an excuse for the Lieutenant, saying he'd been called away.

Katherine took the wallet from Rickenbacher's hand and studied the photo. "If he was older, thinner, had more grey in his hair, he'd be the guy I saw at the hotel."

"You sure?"

"I'm not positive," Katherine said. "This is an old photo, isn't it? You sure look young, but I can still tell it's you. This could be the guy."

"He's a police Lieutenant."

"So?"

Rickenbacher took his wallet back and stared at his former partner's photo for just an instant before folding the wallet closed and slipping it into his pocket. He took Colette aside a few minutes later.

"We've got to get her out of town."

"How?" Colette asked. "You said Castellano's watching the building."

"He can't sit out there all the time. He has to return to the office sooner or later. I'll distract him. You just get her out of here, put her on a bus home."

Rickenbacher emptied the contents of his wallet onto the kitchen table. "This should be enough for the ticket."

"If it's not, I'll cover the difference," Colette said.

Rickenbacher stared deep into the cellar of his soul and saw only darkness. Perhaps he had become one of them, perhaps he had never not been one of them. Still, he knew what he had to do and he prepared for it.

He went outside, located Castellano's car, and then slid into the passenger seat. He said, "I need an address."

When Rickenbacher told him whose, Castellano recited it from memory.

"How long were we partners?" Rickenbacher asked.

"Seventeen years," Castellano said. "Eight in uniform, nine in plain clothes."

"We ever keep any secrets?"

Castellano laughed. "Too many."

"We ever keep any from each other?"

Castellano's laughter died. "Why?"

Rickenbacher slid out of the unmarked car without answering the question.

Rickenbacher cornered Sergeant Kowalski as he came off shift. "You got a picture of that dead girl, Jane Doe 43?"

"The Ainsworth girl?" Kowalski asked. "It's in the file."

Rickenbacher followed the Sergeant through the squad room to Lieutenant Castellano's office.

"Why's the file in here?"

Kowalski shrugged. "The Lieutenant's got a personal interest in this one."

Rickenbacher dropped into Castellano's chair while Kowalski spread the file folder open on the Lieutenant's desk. Sheriff Bubba Rogers had faxed a photo of the missing teenager, then followed it up with a Federal Express overnight package containing the girl's dental records, medical records, and an 8"x10" glossy taken at the local Wal-Mart three months before she disappeared.

Rickenbacher stared at the photo, then glanced up at the two framed photographs adorning Lieutenant Castellano's desk. Except for the retainer Castellano's sister wore, the two girls could have been twins. A moment later he closed the folder and shoved it back into the top center drawer of the Lieutenant's desk.

"You see what you needed?"

Rickenbacher didn't answer the question. Instead, he asked his own. "Where was Castellano when Johnson died?"

"The guy you knocked through his window?"

"He tripped," Rickenbacher corrected.

"The Lieutenant was here, in his office, when the call came through."

"Doing what?"

"Paperwork."

"And after?"

"Home, I suppose," Kowalski said. "He certainly didn't come back to the station."

Rickenbacher sat silently for a moment as he stared at the two photographs on his former partner's desk. "I need you to check a couple more things for me, the duty roster and the shift reports for that night."

"What am I looking for?"

Rickenbacher told the sergeant, then waited until Kowalski returned with the answers to his questions. He said, "Call the Lieutenant back here."

"Haven't I done enough already?" Kowalski protested. "I've been off the clock for half an hour now."

"Tell him you've got some new information about the Jane Doe."

"What?"

"Another witness. Somebody from his past."

"Who?"

"When Castellano gets here, tell him there are no more secrets." When Kowalski looked him a question, Rickenbacher continued. "Tell him that's what I said. He'll understand."

Kowalski radioed the Lieutenant as Rickenbacher headed for the door.

The Fuzzy Clam made the Muff Inn look like the Taj Mahal. For $20, the dancers performed handjobs under the tables in back, and when Rickenbacher went in, he spotted

Walston sitting with a pug-faced brunette who had both hands under the table. He'd removed his glasses and they lay on the table next to a half-empty C.C.-and-Seven.

Rickenbacher waited until Walston stiffened and the brunette brought her hands into view a moment later. Walston fumbled with his zipper, recognized Rickenbacher, and, as soon as he'd tucked himself back into his pants, he invited the big man to join him. Rickenbacher could well imagine what had stained the underside of that table and he declined the invitation. Walston finally joined him at the bar.

"I've got something of yours."

"Yeah?"

"A package that didn't get delivered."

Walston looked him a question, then said, "I'm not missing anything."

"You were working some kind of deal that night, weren't you?"

"I'm working every night."

"Three packages left Gloria's, but only two were delivered. The one I have was intended for Johnson." It contained photographic prints of adolescent and pre-pubescent boys and girls doing things that even Rickenbacher had trouble imagining. "What was in the others?"

Walston motioned the bartender over and had his drink freshened. Then he told Rickenbacher, "You're about to stick your nose in where it doesn't belong, but I'll be as straight with you as I can."

Rickenbacher waited while Walston tried to compose his thoughts. "There's a guy who operates a hit-and-run photo developing operation. He'll develop film or make prints for anybody, things no legit operation would touch. He opens up for a week, then closes back down."

"What'd you get from him?"

"That's the place your nose don't belong," Walston said. He lifted his C.C.-and-Seven and took a sip.

The music changed as one dancer left the stage and another replaced her.

"What about Johnson?"

"Nobody liked what he did, but the photo developer isn't too picky about his clients. Now that Johnson's out of business, I've encouraged the guy to be a little more particular about who he works for."

"No more kiddie stuff?"

Walston shook his head. "Never again."

After a moment's reflection, Rickenbacher asked, "Gilly Boy Thomas working for you?"

"Yeah."

"He been around lately?"

Walston shook his head. "Said he had an accident. Pulled something in his groin."

Rickenbacher nodded thoughtfully. He looked up at the dancer on the stage behind the bar, a pug-faced brunette with sagging water-balloon breasts and a paucity of pubic hair who'd been slathered with glistening oil. She wrapped herself around a polished brass fireman's pole and slid up and down. "You miss him if he's gone?"

"Not particularly," Walston said. "There's a dozen to take his place."

"Keep that in mind," Rickenbacher said, "anything happens to him."

Walston motioned for the bartender as Rickenbacher stood to leave.

Rickenbacher found a pay phone at Good Eats and dialed Colette's number. When she answered, he asked, "Katherine gone?"

"On the bus an hour ago."

"Good."

"I had to damn near beat Bleach to keep him away. He

thought Katherine was a fine, fine looking woman. He told me he had a guy would pay big money for her and offered to split it with me if I'd offer her up," Colette said. "Then he pulled a photo from his pocket. I nearly laughed my ass off when he showed it to me. It was the same one you've been showing around town. A day late and a dollar short, I told him."

Rickenbacher listened to Colette's entire story, then said, "I have something important to do tonight. I need somebody to know what's happening in case it goes wrong." He briefly explained what he had planned.

"Be careful," Colette told him. "Dead men don't get laid."

Rickenbacher drove to the bus station after talking to Colette and he found Bleach leaning against a wooden bench talking to a blonde who couldn't have been older than fourteen. He saw Rickenbacher approaching and stepped away from the young woman to meet him halfway across the station.

"I found your girl," Bleach said. "But some hard-ass 'ho put her on a bus to her mama."

Rickenbacher told the mulatto pimp that he knew all about it and that he had other things to discuss. "The night the Ainsworth girl died, you see anybody familiar in the neighborhood?"

"You mean Nikki?" Bleach asked. "I ain't talking to you none."

"Look," Rickenbacher said, "you already rolled over on Canfield and he isn't going to be real pleased with you when he gets out. You help me now, I'll let him know about it."

"So?"

"I found two winos and a hooker who say they saw a plainclothes detective in the neighborhood the night Nikki died. What'd you see?"

"You want me to roll over on a cop? You out your fuckin'

mind?" Bleach turned to walk away. He stopped when Rickenbacher placed a large hand on his shoulder.

"Did you see any cops that night?"

Bleach turned back around. "None."

"You sure?"

Bleach shrugged. "The street was empty. Wasn't nobody on it but me and Paul and Nikki."

Rickenbacher swore.

Bleach thought for a moment. "Saw an unmarked car, though. It passed by while we's negotiatin'."

"How'd you know what it was?"

"Unmarked cars the most obvious things in the world. Whip antennas and gov'mint plates, what else they be?"

"And?"

"He jus' pass us by like we invisible."

"Thanks," Rickenbacher said.

On his way out, Bleach called to him. "Maybe next time I find the girl fo' you."

Rickenbacher carried the .22 he'd lifted off the poodle-hating boy on his street corner. He entered Gilly Boy's house quietly, made his way to the bedroom, and flipped back the top sheet to reveal the bandages at Gilly Boy's crotch. Then he gently shook the greasy blond awake. Gilly Boy recognized Rickenbacher, remembered him from the first three times he'd been busted.

"Jesus Christ!" he swore as he tried to sit upright. Rickenbacher kept a heavy hand pressed against Gilly Boy's chest, holding him down. His other hand contained a .22 and Gilly Boy stared up the barrel. "The Lieutenant said you'd be coming after me."

"What else did he say?"

Gilly Boy's switchblade lay on his night stand, easily within reach. He knew exactly where he'd left it and didn't have to look for it. "He wanted me to I.D. the guy he says was in the room with the dead girl."

"Canfield?"

"Christ, I don't know the guy's name."

Gilly Boy's hand suddenly darted out to the night stand and came back with his knife. As it swung through the air toward Rickenbacher's throat, the blade snicked open.

Rickenbacher jerked his head backward to avoid the blade, then he backhanded Gilly Boy with the barrel of the pistol, slicing open the blond's cheek with the site.

Gilly Boy tried to kick away the tangle of sheets around his ankles and sit up at the same time, but he couldn't. Rickenbacher grabbed Gilly Boy's wrist and crushed it in his thick hand.

The switchblade fell uselessly to the carpeted floor.

Rickenbacher pushed Gilly Boy back down on the bed.

"There's one more thing."

"Yeah? What's that?"

"Jesse."

Rickenbacher held the barrel of the .22 against Gilly Boy's right eye and pulled the trigger. The gun made a quiet pop, Gilly Boy's eye exploded in a rush of pulp and blood, and the slug exited through the back of his head, through the pillow, through the mattress, finally stopping somewhere in the box spring.

Gilly Boy's body jerked with a spasm, then his bladder and his bowels cut loose.

Rickenbacher smiled. He reached down and retrieved the brass shell ejected from the pistol, picking it up carefully so he didn't burn his fingers.

The smile disappeared when he turned. Gilly Boy's mother stood in the doorway, a gnarled old woman in a tattered pink bathrobe.

"You weren't so quiet, you know."

Rickenbacher shrugged.

"I can't see your face," she said. "I don't know who you are." She stepped aside. "I'm going back to my room now. When I wake up in the morning, I'll call the police."

He heard the old woman shuffle down the hallway, then heard a door close. Sure that Gilly Boy's mother had returned to her bedroom, Rickenbacher let himself out of the house.

Rickenbacher returned home, saw the blinking light on his answering machine, and hit the rewind button. Two hang-ups followed a pre-recorded pitch for vinyl siding, then his former partner's voice caught his attention. "I talked to Kowalski. Now I need to talk to you. I'll be at home, waiting."

Rickenbacher popped the tape from his machine so it wouldn't be recorded over and slipped it into his jacket pocket as he hurried downstairs to his van. Fifteen minutes later he found Castellano's front door open and the Lieutenant in his kitchen. He wore a freshly starched white shirt, a thin black tie held in place with a gold tie chain, black slacks with a razor-sharp crease, and a pair of Italian loafers. He'd shaved recently and had his hair combed neatly into place. A photograph of Castellano's younger sister had been taken from the living room wall and it lay face-up on the table between them. Beside the picture lay a switchblade. Also on the table were an open bottle of Jim Beam and two tumblers, one empty and one containing three fingers of bourbon. The kitchen smelled of bourbon and Lysol and stale sperm. The Lieutenant had Nicolette Ainsworth's missing red shoe in one hand, his service revolver in the other.

"It's about time you got here."

"I had something else to do tonight." Rickenbacher straddled a kitchen chair opposite his former partner.

"You visit Gilly Boy?"

"I sent him to hell," Rickenbacher said. "One-way trip."

Castellano used the barrel of his revolver to push the empty tumbler toward Rickenbacher. "Have a drink," he said, "a toast for the dead."

"Some people deserve to die," Rickenbacher said. "I won't say a toast for them."

Castellano smiled. "So when did you figure it out?"

"A few hours ago."

Castellano placed Nicolette Ainsworth's red spike-heel shoe on the table and lifted the tumbler of bourbon to his lips. He swallowed all three fingers, then poured another three fingers into the tumbler. "You sure you don't want any?"

Rickenbacher shook his head.

"How'd you figure it?"

"After talking to me, you spent some time looking around Johnson's office, maybe kicking up the carpeting near his desk before the lab boys showed up."

Castellano smiled.

"Everybody thinks you went straight home after that. I figure you went for a drive, saw Bleach and Canfield and the girl together."

"Just a glance."

"She looked a lot like Maria, didn't she?"

"I told Maria not to dress like that."

Rickenbacher glared a question at his former partner

"The little slut. Think what she was doing to the family." Castellano used his free hand to lift the tumbler to his lips. He drained it and poured himself another three fingers.

"Is that why you followed Canfield and the girl?"

"I caught her one day. She used to change clothes after she left home, change again on her way home. My parents never knew."

"So what'd you do, follow them to the hotel and wait until Canfield left?"

"Nobody saw me."

"They saw your car."

"My car? I got rid of the car. Traded it in two weeks later. You remember the T-Bird, don't you?"

"They saw your unmarked car. The same one that's sitting in your driveway." Castellano's eyes had glazed over and Rickenbacher knew they weren't discussing the same event. Still, he pressed on. "There was an unmarked car in the neighborhood. Kowalski checked the duty roster and the shift reports for me. There weren't any unmarked cars assigned to the Grafenberg's neighborhood that night. Only an off-duty cop could have taken an unmarked car into the neighborhood."

Castellano knocked his empty tumbler to the floor and grabbed the Jim Beam bottle by the neck. He took a long swallow.

"She was a slut, doing it with all the boys after school. I caught her. I told her to stop. I even threatened her. She just laughed at me. She laughed and she laughed and she laughed."

"So you killed her?"

Castellano sobered up for a moment. His eyes narrowed to slits and he stared across the table at his former partner. "You think I killed my sister?"

"She'd been stabbed to death."

"She wouldn't die. She just kept laughing. Then she came back. And she kept coming back."

"There were others?"

"I made them go away."

"Go away? Go away, where?"

"Home. I sent them home."

"How many others?"

"Too many," Castellano explained. "I sent them home but more of them kept coming every day. They come into the city by bus, they hitch-hike, they come by train. They don't have any money and they wind up in the strip clubs and on the street corners and people like Johnson and Bleach and Canfield and all the others use them and abuse them and there isn't enough milk cartons in the world for all their pictures."

The two former partners sat silent for a long time. The only sound in the room was the splashing of bourbon inside the Jim Beam bottle when Castellano lifted it to his lips and took one long swallow after another. When he'd finally emptied the bottle, Castellano said, "I'm not going down for this. You know what they'll do to a cop inside, don't you?"

"How do you plan to get out of it?"

The Lieutenant lifted his service revolver and placed the barrel in his mouth, the site notched between his teeth. He cocked the hammer back.

Rickenbacher glared at his former partner. "So what are you waiting for, my sympathy? Pull the trigger, you spic fuck."

Castellano squeezed the trigger, the report of the gun echoing in the tiny kitchen nearly deafening Rickenbacher. When the big man opened his eyes, the back of Castellano's head had been blown out and his brains were splattered across the stainless steel sink and the wall behind it. Castellano's service revolver slipped from his lifeless hand and fell to the floor.

Rickenbacher stared at the dead body for a few minutes, then he pulled the .22 from his boot, carefully wiped his fingerprints off, and pressed it into the dead man's hand, impressing the Lieutenant's fingerprints on the gun that had killed Gilly Boy Thomas.

Carefully, so as not to disturb anything else in the room, he slipped the .22 into the waistband of the Lieutenant's pants, at the small of his back.

Then he made two phone calls, one to Sergeant Kowalski's home number and a second to 911.

Kowalski questioned Rickenbacher, listened to the tape from Rickenbacher's answering machine, then questioned him again. At first he couldn't believe what he'd just been told about Lieutenant Castellano, but later when the blood-type from the semen found inside Nicolette Ainsworth's red spike-heeled shoe matched the Lieutenant's blood-type, Kowalski ordered a confirming DNA test.

"Why'd he do it?" Kowalski repeatedly asked Rickenbacher, but the big man didn't have an answer.

Another day would pass before he tied the .22 in the Lieutenant's waistband to the death of Gilly Boy Thomas, and after he did, Kowalski didn't bother to investigate further.

Chapter 12

After he'd been released, Paul Canfield met Rickenbacher at the Muff Inn and slipped him an envelope filled with cash. "Nice job."

"It isn't over yet." Rickenbacher pocketed the money, straightened his hat and slipped out through the rear.

Two hours later Ben Kirkland earned four hundred dollars for breaking both of Canfield's kneecaps. The only thing

Canfield heard from Kirkland was, "Don't ever touch jailbait again."

When Rickenbacher told Jesse about it later, he left out most of the details. Still, she asked, "What gives you the right to play God?"

"Gilly Boy wrote his own ticket," Rickenbacher said. "I just punched it for him."

Jesse stared at him for a long, long time. She'd wished Gilly Boy Thomas dead and he'd died. Rickenbacher had killed him as easily as she turned off a light.

"You've changed," she finally said. "You're not the same man you were all those years ago. I'm not sure I can live with the knowledge of what you've done."

Rickenbacher understood. Three strikes, he was out. He pushed himself out of the chair and went to the door, standing with his big hand wrapped around the knob and waiting for her to say something else.

She didn't.

Rickenbacher phoned Colette and told her everything had worked out. "There's one thing I forgot to ask."

"What's that?"

"How's your niece?"

"In therapy."

"She going to be okay?"

"She will now. Her bastard father skipped town after my sister served him with divorce papers. Her lawyer threatened to press child molestation charges, too."

"He likely to come back?"

She hesitated. "I don't think so."

"He ever shows up, you call me, okay?"

"The first number I dial," she said. "That's a promise."

That night, Rickenbacher sat on his couch in his underwear, a bottle of Budweiser in one hand and an opened *TV Guide* in the other. He let the phone ring twice before he answered it. On the other end of the line, Hubert Cove said, "My daughter's home and we've had a long talk. She told me what you did for her."

"You all right with everything?" Rickenbacher asked.

"Not really, but she's my daughter. I'll learn." At that moment, Rickenbacher thought he might learn to like Cove.

When their brief conversation ended, Rickenbacher placed the phone's handset in its cradle and turned up the volume on his portable black-and-white television. *Dragnet* had just begun.

As Joe Friday began detailing his day in the Rampart Division, Rickenbacher's doorbell rang. He pushed himself from the couch and crossed the room. When he pulled the door open, he found himself staring down at Jesse.

"I don't want to lose you again," she said.

Rickenbacher pulled her into his arms and they kissed long and hard.

About the Author

Michael Bracken is the author of *Bad Girls, Deadly Campaign, Even Roses Bleed, In the Town of Dreams Unborn and Memories Dying, Just in Time for Love, Psi Cops, Tequila Sunrise*, and more than 700 shorter works published in Australia, Canada, China, England, Ireland, and the United States. He was born in Canton, Ohio, has traveled extensively throughout the U.S., and currently resides in Waco, Texas, with his wife, Sharon, and his son, Ian. He has three other children — Ryan, Courtney, and Nigel — from a previous marriage.

www.ingramcontent.com/pod-product-compliance
Lightning Source LLC
Chambersburg PA
CBHW05075225062 6
47155CB00005B/2025